ORWELL'S LUCK

Orwell's Luck

Richard Jennings

Houghton Mifflin Company Boston
Walter Lorraine Books

Walter Lorraine ⓦ Books

Text copyright © 2000 by Richard Jennings

Library of Congress Cataloging-in-Publication Data

Jennings, Richard W. (Richard Walker), 1945-
  Orwell's Luck / by Richard W. Jennings.
      p. cm.
  Summary: While caring for an injured rabbit which
becomes her confidant, horoscope writer, and source of good
luck, a thoughtful seventh grade girl learns to see things in
more than one way.
  ISBN 0-618-03628-8
  [1. Rabbits—Fiction. 2. Horoscopes—Fiction] I. Title.

PZ7.J4298765 or 2000
[Fic]—dc21
                                              99-033501

Printed in the United States of America
QUM 10 9 8 7 6 5 4 3 2

For Philip, Alex, and Mary

ORWELL'S LUCK

Home delivery

All my life, I have been a person who wakes up with the birds. They say the early bird gets the worm, and I suppose it's true, but what gets me out of bed is not worms, but the opportunity to be the first one in my family to get to the newspaper.

The newspaper contains the comics, and, more importantly, the comics pages contain the daily horoscope guide. This is vital information. I can't imagine getting through the day without it.

On this particular day, the first day of a brand-new year, when I made the dash across the frost-covered lawn while the rest of my family slept, I was startled to discover a brown rabbit sprawled unhappily atop the fat, plastic-wrapped holiday paper.

He held his head erect. His eyes were bright. His ears turned in my direction like satellite dishes. His nose twitched in that reassuring manner unique to rabbits. But his hindquarters were as lifeless as the laundry hidden beneath my bed. As I stood over him assessing the situation, he thrashed his forefeet about, which served only to turn him in circles.

It appeared that I was confronted with yet another victim of urban carelessness, an event possibly perpetrated by the driver of the newspaper truck, a man I had never met, but who, I suspected, associated high speeds with professional achievement. The evidence lay at my bare feet, which were turning uncomfortably cold.

I surveyed the surrounding front lawns, just in case this madman somehow had managed to dispose of an entire rabbit family in a single blow, but this was the only crippled creature in sight. The rabbit's discomfort, and mine, prompted me to remove him to warmer surroundings. I unrolled the newspaper, fashioned it into a makeshift gurney, and carried him into the kitchen, where I placed him on the countertop.

"Don't be scared," I said, as if he could understand my words. "I like rabbits."

I looked him over. He wasn't bleeding and there were no bones sticking out. Whatever his problem was, it was inside, not outside.

Since I didn't know what else to do, I just talked to him, hoping that would make him feel better.

"Do you have a name?" I asked him.

He looked at me sadly in silence.

"Well, you need one," I told him. "If only to make the conversation go more smoothly."

First I thought about calling him Star, after the newspaper by the same name, but that sounded too much like something a kid would come up with. Then I tried out some more imaginative stuff, names that would signify his special status of being the first terrorist victim of the year, but TERREX-A and VIC-001 sounded like the government was involved. Even the perfectly innocent and popular name Thumper, which you'd think would be OK, seemed in bad taste under the circumstances.

Finally, I settled on the name Orwell, because, like all good names, it just seemed to fit.

A room of his own

Orwell had not only arrived as a harbinger of the new year, he had come at a critical time in my personal career. I had recently turned twelve, and was well into the first half of seventh grade at a brand-new school, where instead of being one of the oldest kids knowing all the ropes, like I had been in sixth

ound myself one of the youngest kids know-
opes at all. That's why I was considering
ering the field of private investigations, after
school and on weekends, or maybe becoming an
explorer like Lewis or Clark. I also liked shooting
baskets in my driveway, which is where I had come
up with these plans.

Like himself, the house that Orwell entered was
damaged in the back. My father had approved my
mother's remodeling scheme, and thanks to an ever-
changing team of workmen, the back of our mid-
western bungalow was torn away, leaving boards
and pipes exposed, with only loosely fastened sheets
of thin blue plastic separating our living space from
the skeletal rooms-in-progress beyond. As a result, it
was chilly in the kitchen that morning — no place for
an injured rabbit to recuperate.

Not only that, but when the other members of my
family got up, they were sure to be hungry, cranky,
and outspoken about their objections to encounter-
ing wild animals in the food service area. My mother, I suspected, would take the horrified view of a
public health inspector. My sister would vacillate
between the feeling that rabbits are cute, and the
realization that this one, in its present damaged form,
was "too sad." My father's verdict was unpredictable.

To avoid a family quarrel, I decided to move
Orwell once again, this time to the relative safety of

the unfinished master bathroom. The plumbing fixtures were inoperative, but the heat was on and the door could be closed. Everything in the room was covered with a fine layer of construction dust, so I spread open the front page of the paper in the new ceramic tub and gently placed the rabbit on the clean newsprint.

It made a fine nesting place.

The household awakes

Apart from the risks associated with the introduction of a wounded wild rabbit into a household made up of four highly independent people, there were also the dog and the cat to consider.

I mention the dog first because he joined us first, as a puppy many years ago, when we were a young family on the way up. He is of mixed pedigree, half Pomeranian and half poodle, a combination that gives you an obedient, curly-haired creature about the size and shape of a pig.

Now generally ignored by the people who picked him out, the dog sleeps in the house at night and surveys his fenced kingdom in the backyard by day. He lives well enough, I suppose. His diet consists of tuna, cheddar cheese, baked chicken, and sweet-and-sour pork from the Imperial Garden, bolstered by the occasional interlude of canned Lucky Dog and

Science City diet pellets, food he rarely eats but is there anyway, just in case.

The fact is, the pellets are consumed each morning by the blue jays, starlings, and other feathered camp-followers who come to drink at the goldfish pond, and the Lucky Dog sustains the scavengers housed in and around the woodpile. Whenever the dog's bowl is empty, my father barks at me, "Feed the dog!" What we are doing, of course, is feeding the birds, the mice, and the occasional visiting possum.

The cat is my sister's. Within the house, they go everywhere together.

In considering the family pets, it occurred to me that if their natural instincts should ever, by some miracle, return, it could affect Orwell's chances for getting better. A debilitated rabbit would be an easy meal for a less well fed dog and cat. Even as sport, Orwell could provide fine high jinks for a couple of bored household carnivores.

For the time being, I thought it best to refrain from advertising Orwell's existence and the location of his hideout. Mum was the word of the day.

While my family performed their morning rituals upstairs, I located some supplies left over from a sixth-grade science fair project. From a one-liter glass beaker, a drip valve, a strip of plastic tubing, and a metal stand, I assembled a contraption that would provide Orwell with nourishment on an as-needed basis.

I filled the container with a nutritional mush made from pulverized Science City diet pellets mixed with bottled water. I forced the tubing past the rabbit's amazingly sharp incisors. This was not only difficult, it was a mistake. The little guy bit me, making a deep and bloody cut in my forefinger, which I treated with antibiotic ointment and sterile gauze. I made a mental note to find out later about rabies, tetanus, and rabbit fever. I also found a pair of heavy leather gloves. Ironically, the gloves were lined with rabbit fur.

Orwell seemed willing enough to consume the dog food mush, a good sign for a creature I feared was on death's doorstep. I closed the door to the bathroom and joined my family in the kitchen for a satisfying breakfast of thawed waffles soaked in syrup and topped with sliced bananas. I kept my bandaged finger in my pocket.

"You've taken the comics again!" my sister accused me.

"What in the world has happened to the front page?" my mother complained. "This is so irritating!"

"Must we?" my father sighed, looking up from the Help Wanted ads. My father always read the Help Wanted ads because my father disliked his job. Turning to me, he said, "If you're going to read the newspaper before anyone else, please have the courtesy to reassemble it."

I quietly excused myself, leaving my sticky plate, glass, and silverware in the middle of the kitchen table surrounded by strands and globs of maple-flavored syrup. Later, this would launch a general discussion on household responsibilities, eventually concluding with my mother and my father ignoring me, while continuing to debate the subject between themselves.

"It's just her age," my mother would maintain, while my father, taking it upon himself to clear my breakfast dishes, would suggest that absent-mindedness was a genetic flaw I had inherited, possibly from my mother's mother. It would be a momentary skirmish, an airing of opposing views. Strictly routine stuff.

A member of the family

Orwell's new home was more like a church sanctuary than a rabbit hutch. Separated from the rest of the house by a minefield of fallen nails, discarded two-by-fours, plaster rocks, long-forgotten soda cans, and other worker's flotsam, the new master bathroom was a wonderful place to be alone with one's thoughts and one's rabbit.

There was a skylight over the raised bathtub, a double vanity, a shower, a heat lamp, and several illuminated sconces controlled by a dimmer switch. A long mirror had been installed over the twin sinks, and another, opposite it, over the tub. The floor by the shower was covered with handmade tiles from Italy. On the rest of the floor, deep wool carpeting snuggled your feet. The wallpaper had been custom-made to complete the effect, and the effect, in my view, was like being at the altar of the Hedge Grove United Methodist Church, where my family and I sometimes attended services.

Lying reverently in the center of it all was Orwell. He raised his head when I entered, but he exhibited no fear. Remembering to wear my gloves, I offered him a stolen piece of celery. He needed coaxing at first, but soon began gnawing at it greedily. As he ate, I stroked the back of his tiny head. He lay his ears back to accommodate me. I was careful not to touch his spine.

As we both became more comfortable, I removed the glove from my right hand and felt his soft chest. There was a strong, rapid heartbeat. I gently pinched his back feet to try to determine if he was more than half a rabbit. He responded with a slight wiggle in his shoulders. I held his feet one at a time. They were warm, like the rest of him.

It appeared that life was flowing through Orwell, but any notion of rabbit's feet being talismans for good fortune was dispelled by the sad sight of this helpless, crumpled creature. I guessed that his pelvis had been broken, probably by a glancing blow from the wheels of the newspaper truck. Even if he had a chance to live, he could be crippled for life.

Looking at him lying so still in the natural spotlight created by the skylight above him, my heart went out to this unlucky little rabbit. Whatever was to become of him, I realized, was up to me.

As a family, even though we do go to church sometimes, the meaning of life is not always on our minds. But somehow Orwell had found his way to me, and therein lay a duty that I could not deny. Maybe he'd dragged himself for miles to get to my house. Maybe the word was out among the forlorn, the homeless, and the wounded that here was a house with a soft touch, a house where the Science City diet pellets and the Lucky Dog flowed in a magical endless stream.

This is not a bad reputation to have.

"I thought you seemed quiet at breakfast," my father said. Somehow he had sniffed out my hideout. He was still dressed in his bathrobe, his eyeglasses were crooked, his hair was in disarray, and he needed a shave. Had he not been my father, he would have frightened me.

"I found him this morning, in the front yard," I explained.

"He's a handsome one," my father said. "Goes well with the colors of the bathroom, too. That should please your mother."

He knelt to examine Orwell. "Looks like his back is broken," he said. "Or his pelvis. Either way, he's a goner. Wild rabbits have a tough row to hoe, no matter where they live."

I guess he saw the look on my face, because his voice softened when he added, "I don't mean to criticize your work. It looks like you've done all anybody can do. But don't get your hopes up."

"I think he may have a chance," I said. I explained how Orwell had responded.

"Well, until we know what the damage is, all you can do is keep him warm, try to feed him, and keep him away from predators. Funny thing about rabbits, about the only thing they can do to protect themselves is run away. They're usually very good at running away. This one, however, is not. *Ergo*, a goner."

"But surely there's something we can do!" I protested.

"Not on a Sunday. All the animal hospitals are closed. Tomorrow's out, too. Federal holiday. But the first thing Tuesday, if he's still alive, we'll pack him up and take him to the vet."

"Thanks," I said.

"By the way, does this creature have a name?" he asked.

"Orwell. I named him Orwell."

"That's too bad," my father observed, preparing to

leave the room. "Once they have a name, they become part of the family. It's always harder when you lose a member of the family."

Idle pursuits

My mother's position in the household was too important to keep her in the dark about Orwell for long. I was pleased that my father chose to break the ice for me.

"Of course the rabbit will have to go," he told her. "But it is a situation that will take care of itself. His days are numbered."

"I will not have animals living in my bathroom," my mother said.

"You'll probably get your wish very soon," he replied.

"Isn't there some place you can take it?" she implored him.

"Surely you can adapt," he said.

After a troubling pause, during which my mother gave my father that familiar, menacing flash from her eyes that he calls "house lightning," she took a deep breath and finally said, "Oh, all right. But please don't let it get anything on the wallpaper."

The remainder of that winter day was spent in idle pursuits.

My grandmother, my mother's widowed mother

who lives nearby, dropped in to visit, which was unusual since she usually waited until my father was gone someplace. She brought cookies for everybody.

My father and I watched an old black-and-white movie about a detective who figures out that the black falcon statue a dying man delivers to his office is really made of solid gold. Everybody was after it, but the movie was mostly just people talking.

I watched another movie about the luckiest kid on earth, a boy my age who wins the lottery and uses the money to buy his school so he can be the boss. It was excellent.

Then I played Scrabble with my sister, a long game that I finally won, thanks to the skillful and creative spelling of a few guttural sounds that I convinced her were fragments of early human speech, plus an unexpected late-game break that gave me "X-ray" on a Triple Word Score.

"Luck of the draw," my father observed when my sister began to complain.

At appropriate intervals, I worked the feeding tube for Orwell and gently stroked his shoulders and that bumpy part behind his ears. He seemed to like the attention, but I felt really sorry for him.

"Please don't die," I begged him. "It's no way to start out a friendship."

That night, as I was sliding groggily into sleep, I realized that in all of the day's excitement, I hadn't looked at my horoscope! The first day of a brand-new year and I had forgotten to check!

I pulled the covers up over my head. Whatever it was that fate had in store for me, it was too late to do anything about it now.

So far, so good

Orwell didn't die. He made it through the night, and maybe it was just my optimistic imagination, but he seemed to be perkier than the day before. Equally reassuring was the message in the newspaper's daily horoscope guide for Monday.

Horoscopes give you the lay of the land for an entire twenty-four hours in one short, simple phrase. If good things are destined to happen to you that day, you can be ready to receive them with open arms. On the other hand, if bad things are in store, you can be on your guard. Either way, you know what to expect.

The horoscope messages in the newspaper are hidden from the casual reader. They consist of twelve tiny boxes, one for each sign of the zodiac, with each box containing seven numbers and a little circular moon.

Depending on what kind of day you're going to have, the moon wears a smile face or a frown face, or, if your day is "neutral," it has no face, but is presented as half dark and half light. Between the two vertical rows of message boxes is a long list of words that correspond to all the numbers. To find out what's going to happen to you, you must first decode the message.

I am a Scorpio, like my father — *exactly* like my father, since fate long ago decreed in a curious coincidence that we share the same autumn birthday. The horoscope for Scorpio had a moon with a smile face and seven numbers that I hurried to decipher.

The first word was "take." I looked up the next one. It was "friend." Then came "to," followed by "exclusive" and "restaurant." In my haste, I almost made a mistake on the next word. At first I thought it was "explode," which gave me a start, but then I realized that I was looking at the word above the word for me. My word was "treat." The last word was actually two words stuck together. It was "him/her."

TAKE FRIEND TO EXCLUSIVE RESTAURANT
TREAT HIM/HER.

Huh? I didn't get it. What did this have to do with a broken rabbit in my mother's not-quite-finished new bathroom?

Then it came to me. Of course! The friend was Orwell. And at this very moment he was the only customer in the most exclusive restaurant in town — my place! I was already doing what the horoscope recommended! I was not only on track, I was a little

15

bit ahead. No wonder the stars gave me a smile face moon!

The Monday holiday passed into history. Two days of the new year had been encountered and survived by all, Orwell included. There was still the matter of the medical evaluation to deal with, but so far, so good, I figured. So far, so good.

Luck of the draw

My father's willingness to make the trip to the animal hospital, in spite of his forecast of Orwell's doom, was a good sign. Even better, he didn't seem to mind my being late for school after such a long holiday break.

With a hopeful heart, I searched for more encouragement in Scorpio's horoscope for Tuesday, the third day of the year. Decorated with the face of a smiling moon, the encryption when decoded said

CONCENTRATE ON MECHANICAL REPAIRS
ENJOY AMUSEMENTS TONIGHT.

I double-checked my deciphering because, once again, the horoscope did not make much sense to me. The smile face made it seem good, and the word "enjoy" was a welcome ingredient, but what sort of "mechanical repairs" and "amusements" did the stars have in mind? After giving my brain a workout, I finally decided they must be talking about getting Orwell's legs fixed. Repairs like that would provide plenty of amusement later on.

Equipped with these astrological insights, I was feeling pretty cheerful by the time we walked into the animal hospital.

I don't know why they call them animal "hospitals." They're really just little office buildings with a few tables and pens in various sizes, more like pet stores than hospitals. This one was called Family Pet Care.

I waited restlessly for the veterinarian to finish examining a cat that was one can of Chicken of the Sea over the line, followed by a big red Irish setter that was being vaccinated for the latest in dog diseases.

I cradled Orwell in my arms, being careful to situate myself so that his lifeless legs would rest gently against my thighs. My father leafed distractedly through the pages of a fashion magazine. Then it was our turn.

The veterinarian appeared to be surprised by the purpose of our visit. "Wild rabbits don't have much of a chance," he said.

At my father's insistence, the veterinarian took X-rays anyway. They looked like the amateur snapshots that some people take where they accidentally cut off their subjects' heads. You could see Orwell's bones from his shoulders down. There was a top view. There was a side view. But nobody bothered to get a picture of his face, his best feature.

The X-rays proved to be evidence of nothing more than the fact that some creatures have extremely small bones. The good news was that none of them appeared to be broken.

"It could be spinal cord injury," the veterinarian speculated.

"Does that mean he'll recover?" I asked.

"Well," he answered unconvincingly, "sometimes they do."

He gave Orwell a cortisone shot. He gave him an antibiotic shot. He gave him shots for all the diseases and conditions that make life hard for the bedridden patient. In less than half an hour, the charges he ran up were equal to the cost of a major household appliance.

"Keep doing what you're doing," he said. "And hope for the best."

This was probably good advice, but I didn't think it was worth that much money. As my father signed the check with his usual illegible scribble, I was discouraged by the veterinarian's cheery confession. "Thanks for coming in," he said. "I've never had a wild rabbit before."

At school that day, all I could think about was Orwell. Nothing had changed. Nothing except that no one could say for certain what was wrong. But

Orwell could not move his back legs. The running part, the kicking part, the getaway part was useless and nobody could tell me why.

That night I couldn't sleep. I got up every hour or so and visited Orwell. I fed him fresh vegetables from my ungloved hand. I stroked him. I talked to him. He looked at me and every once in a while feigned a useless struggle to run away. I cleaned up after him. The new bathroom had begun to smell faintly like Family Pet Care.

The food tube worked exceptionally well. At the veterinarian's suggestion, I had switched from dog food mush to rabbit food mush. Orwell swallowed it right down and clamped his teeth on the plastic tube, hungry for more. I let him have as much as he wanted.

"Hang in there, Orwell," I said. "You still have a chance." I didn't know if this was true. I hoped it wouldn't hurt to say it.

I became angry with the newspaper truck driver. Animal killer! Maimer! Agent of evil! Orwell was just another "whup-thup" sound to him, like a fat newspaper hitting a concrete driveway. That's the kind of thing I was thinking.

During the night my father came to see me. "Get some sleep," he insisted. "I'll take over."

I didn't go right away. We took turns watching, touching, hoping.

"If they're not broken," I asked, "why can't he

move them?"

"Luck of the draw," my father replied.

Was it just bad luck? I wondered. Or was something else involved? Something that actually caused certain days to be good days and certain days to be bad days, like the stars that rule my daily horoscope.

Maybe I was misinterpreting the message in the newspaper. It hadn't been especially clear anyway. I decided I'd better study tomorrow's horoscope more carefully.

As I turned to leave, Orwell looked at me. He raised his head as best he could, and stared at me with those big brown rabbit eyes. I picked him up. I held him to my chest, his lifeless legs dangling, his tiny rabbit heart beating softly against mine.

Deductive reasoning

I woke up Wednesday with two big problems on my mind. The first was school, which, after so much time off for creative loafing and lifesaving, was an unwelcome change of pace. The other problem, of course, was Orwell.

I hurried through my morning routine, getting dressed, letting the dog out, getting the paper, and pouring myself an extra-large bowl of crunchy, sweetened cereal to gulp down while figuring out my horoscope. I wanted to read it first, before I checked on Orwell, just in case it said something like NEW FRIEND PASSES AWAY QUIETLY IN NIGHT. But what it actually said was

TODAY WILL RUN SMOOTHER
THAN YOU ANTICIPATED.

Once again, my horoscope bore the sign of the smiling moon. I was glad about this, of course, and glad, too, that this one was easy to understand, unlike the previous two. But I remained wary, since the other two hadn't exactly panned out. I wondered, Is there a limit to how many smile faces in a row a person can get? How long could my luck — and Orwell's — hold out?

I admit it. I was afraid. I entered Orwell's hideout like I was entering the mummy's tomb. I tiptoed in, shutting my eyes when I opened the door, afraid to look. I didn't open my eyes until I was completely inside and there was no turning back.

The first thing I saw was Orwell looking back at me. He was still alive, thank goodness, awake and alert and hungry for the apple slices I'd brought. He munched happily as I scratched his knobby little head and thought about my personal career.

The day before, while shooting baskets in the driveway, before it got too cold and I had to come inside, I changed my mind about what I wanted to be. I was still interested in becoming a detective, but

21

I was also thinking about being a veterinarian, one who specializes in small animals that people find in their yards, and, unlike some I could name, actually figures out how to fix them. I was also trying to work the trombone into whatever I chose, since I'd recently started playing it at my new school and sort of liked it.

School was not really such a bad place. It just contained too many strangers and lasted too long. My father told me that for him, the worst part about his job was not being able to leave when he wanted to. That's how I feel about being at school. Once you get there, you're stuck like a bunny in a bathtub.

But some parts of school are actually interesting. Like band and science and P.E. Math is OK. Also, I started taking French. I hadn't learned very many French words, but the few I did know made me think that one of the reasons there's more than one way of saying things is because there's more than one way of looking at things.

For example, in English, when we decide it's time to leave, we say, "Let's go!" The French, however, say, "*Allons-y*," which means, "Let's go to the aforementioned place." This little difference between the two languages says to me that the French don't go anywhere unless they know where they're going, but Americans, on the other hand, are happy just to keep moving.

Orwell could not keep moving, and so, I concluded, unless he is French, he must be unhappy.

I tried to imagine what he must have been thinking when he found himself unable to hop and was forced to crawl on his belly, powered only by the strength of his underdeveloped front legs. Did he say to himself, "Let's go!" and then, through sheer luck, wind up here? Or did he think, "Let's go to the aforementioned kid's house"?

When I found Orwell in so exhausted a state, how far had he traveled before pausing to rest, putting a rolled-up newspaper between his tender white belly and the hard, cold, frost-covered ground? Was he trying desperately to get to my door, like a doomed man delivering a newspaper-wrapped falcon to a black-and-white detective? Was Orwell delivering something to me? A message, perhaps?

This is called deductive reasoning. All the best detectives do it. By putting my brain to work doing deductive reasoning, I was able to come up with a few plausible theories.

Theory number one was that Orwell was an accident victim, a hapless rabbit who stepped blithely into the path of a newspaper truck driven by a careless part-time worker in a hurry to get back to bed.

Theory number two was that someone tried to kill Orwell to prevent him from delivering a message.

Then there was theory number three, made up of parts of theories one and two. Theory number three dismissed the injury as an accident, but kept in the part about the message.

The only problem with this line of reasoning was that it led to a very big question — namely, What was the message? Whatever it was, I had a feeling it was going to be a lot tougher to crack than the seven little numbers printed in my daily horoscope guide.

My thoughts were interrupted by a knock on the bathroom door. It was my sister, wearing a smile that looked like the one the stars had been issuing to Scorpio lately. Standing behind her, lined up like they were waiting to buy tickets for a movie, were the two little girls who live next door.

"They want to see Orwell," my sister said.

"Beat it!" I told them. "*Va-t'en!*"

A certain smile

The next day, a frown face on my horoscope made everything go haywire. The prediction for Scorpio began positively enough. "A good day," it said. But by the time I finished decoding the rest of the message, it had turned into

A GOOD DAY TO CUT YOUR LOSSES.

Yikes! I thought. And for good reason.

I got a C on a history paper, my father lost his job,

the construction project on the back of my house was stopped dead in its tracks, and my mother walked around all evening with a goofy look on her face hardly saying a word.

The one good thing about this day was that Orwell didn't die.

After the school bus brought me home, I shot baskets until suppertime. I like the way a basketball feels. Unlike a baseball, a basketball is too big to hold on to for very long. You have to do something with it. You have to keep it moving. If a basketball could talk, it would always be saying, "Let's go!"

After supper, I did my homework with Orwell in his private rabbit hutch. He seemed to be doing OK. He really liked the lettuce leaves my mother had saved for him. In spite of what she sometimes says, deep down inside, my mother has a kind heart.

I tackled my science homework first. Science is an interesting subject. I especially like learning about animals. Take rabbits, for example. A lot of people will try to tell you that rabbits are rodents, like guinea pigs or woodchucks or mice, but they're not. Rabbits are members of the order Lagomorpha. Unlike rodents, they have not one, but two sets of upper front teeth, a little pair behind the big pair. And let me tell you, every one of those front teeth is razor sharp!

There are many kinds of rabbits living all over the

world. The best known is the cottontail. Orwell is a cottontail rabbit. According to my science book, although many rabbits settle in large groups in underground burrows called warrens, cottontail rabbits are different.

Cottontails are "Let's go!" kind of rabbits. They like to stay on the move, spending their days above ground. Their homes are just temporary hiding places in tall grass or bushes. They prefer to be alone and only get together with other rabbits when it's time to eat or to start a family.

I looked up from my notebook. Orwell was watching me. He didn't act scared at all.

"Hey, Orwell," I said. "Was there something you wanted to tell me?"

His ears perked up and he raised his chest up, too, like he was going to stand. But, of course, he couldn't.

"Don't worry, Orwell," I told him. "It'll be all right. My grandmother says that when stuff happens, even when it's bad, it happens for a good reason. It's just that we don't always know what the reason is."

Orwell twitched his nose at me a mile a minute and opened his little pink mouth like he really was going to say something. Then, all of a sudden, he smiled at me. It was really fast, and it only lasted a second, but it was definitely a smile.

A secret signal

Three weeks passed, but nothing changed. Not Orwell. Not my house. Not my father's jobless situation. It was as if time, like an injured rabbit, had simply stopped moving forward.

Each morning, before getting ready for school, I read my horoscope, and each morning it said things like

MAKE GOOD USE OF OPPORTUNITIES PRESENTED YOU

and

RESUME PROJECT YOU HAVE PUT ON HOLD.

Hardly predictions. Not even very good advice. About what you'd expect from the fortune cookies at the Imperial Garden. It seemed that even the stars had slowed down.

And then, quite unexpectedly, my horoscopes began to change. One Monday morning in late January, the seven deciphered numbers in Scorpio spelled out this message:

UNDER NEW MANAGEMENT

WATCH FOR SPECIAL INSTRUCTIONS.

"What kind of horoscope is this?" I asked right out loud.

Starting over at the beginning, I carefully checked every word again. Then I deciphered Pisces and Aries, choosing two strangers at random, to see if their messages were anything like mine. Theirs was the usual stuff:

DRESS FOR SUCCESS TODAY YOU'LL BE GLAD
and
A TELEPHONE CALL BRINGS NEWS FROM AFAR.

This is strange, I thought. But by the time I got to school, I had forgotten all about it.

The next day, my horoscope was at it again, advising

STAY TUNED FOR AN IMPORTANT NEWS BULLETIN.

This is really weird, I thought.

Then, in a complete departure from horoscope protocol, I got the very same message for two more days. Just when I was getting tired of staying tuned, on Friday the repetitive series was broken with these words:

KEEP ALL FURTHER COMMUNICATIONS
UNDER YOUR HAT.

"What in the Sam Hill universe is going on?" I blurted out.

"Watch your language!" my father admonished, barely lifting his eyes from the Help Wanted section.

"I should say so!" my mother agreed.

"Maybe you better go feed the dog," my father instructed.

The dog is older than I am. My parents got him so they could practice taking care of something before they decided to have kids. My mother says it was all my father's idea. She didn't need a dog to tell her if she wanted children. The only thing getting a dog did for her, she says, was convince her that she didn't want a dog. Under the circumstances, I guess I am lucky to have been born.

That night I hung out with Orwell until bedtime. I had come up with a special knock on the door, so he'd know it was me. Three longs, a short, and a long.

Tap-tap-tap-ta-tap!

This was the secret signal, and I was careful not to perform it in the presence of others.

Unfortunately, since Orwell's thumping feet were out of commission, he could not return the signal. But he seemed to like it, because he looked happy when I let myself in.

"Hey, Orwell, what's the good word?" I greeted him, handing him a carrot strip.

While he ate his snack, I cleaned up his habitat and told him about my day at school, what was going on with my father and his job, what my sister was up to, and how my mother was taking everything. I even told him about stuff I'd read in the paper and seen on TV.

Orwell continued munching on carrot strips. Every once in a while he'd rotate his ears or wiggle his nose. But when I mentioned the recent episodes with my horoscope, Orwell stopped what he was doing, sat very still, and looked me in the eyes for the longest time, so long that I was able to see my reflection in them, and not just me, but the whole room, curved and reproduced in miniature — a tiny, magical world displayed in duplicate by two of the brightest, shiniest, brownest eyes I've ever seen.

From the watchtower

On Saturday, I picked up the paper in the rain. It was a gentle, sorrowful rain that began sometime in the middle of the night. Despite its misty quality, by the time I got outside it had created a puddle near the basketball goal. This was a sign that the creek was rising. Soon the outdoor creatures would be moving up the hill toward the safety of the higher ground on which our little house was perched.

The dog wisely went back inside, but I stayed out

to restock the Science City diet pellets and after that tossed out some cornbread left over from supper, plus a brown-spotted apple that Orwell had declined. Then I went back to my room to read the paper.

Saturday's horoscope was the strangest one yet:

BRONCOS TRAMPLE FALCONS 3419
GRAB SECOND RING.

By now, of course, I was expecting it to be a surprise. But I wasn't expecting it to be a code within a code. This one had me stumped. I got up from my desk and sat down on my bed to noodle it over.

My room is on the second floor at the end of the hall. It is the only room in the house that is L-shaped. My desk is in the short part of the L. My bed is in the long part. Along the walls of the long part are bookcases filled with my collections, souvenirs, science equipment, and books. Above the bookcases hangs a framed poster of lightning flashing over the prairie. I don't know where the picture was taken, but it looks a lot like where I live.

In the corner of my room are two windows that meet at right angles. When I sit on the edge of my bed, I can see everything in the backyard — the new addition, the concrete patio, the dog dishes, the goldfish pond, the woodpile, and the hedgeapple tree with the tree house that my father built a long time ago. I can even see over the bushes into the neighborhood park. That corner of my room is my own private watchtower.

It hadn't taken the neighborhood animals long to discover the stash I'd set out. The scavenger birds and half-tame squirrels were already at it. They're always the first to arrive. Soon, however, the shy ones began poking their faces out from the thick honeysuckle hedge. Chipmunks came to the party, darting and dashing across the ground like minnows in a stream. A flock of purple finches, seeing that the braver birds were having a good time, decided it was safe for them to join in. Species by species, a crowd began to form.

Then, fashionably late, a rabbit appeared, a brown rabbit, moving ever so carefully, its radar turned on high beam, listening for warnings from the starlings and jays and sparrows, cautiously waiting for an opportunity to inspect the bounty. It was smaller than Orwell, and not as picky either, because it soon began nibbling the soft, spotted apple that no one else wanted.

Sitting still as a winter tree, I watched the rabbit eat its breakfast. It was darker than Orwell, but maybe that was because it was wet. I tried to get a look at its face, but its back was turned to me.

Suddenly, the rude raspy bark of a neighbor's dog out for a forced walk caused the timid little visitor to leap up, zigzagging across the yard, through the honeysuckle, into the park, and on to some distant hideout far beyond my field of vision.

"*Allez-y!*" I whispered in encouragement. "Go there!"

On Orwell's behalf, I envied this stranger's superb hopping skills. The little creature sure did make it look easy.

I lay back on my bed and closed my eyes. Even though I tried not to think about them, the week's weird horoscope messages flashed on and off in my mind, like insistent little neon signs.

I also thought about giving up my plans for becoming a detective. Figuring things out was becoming too hard. It occurred to me to become a weather forecaster instead. I really like weather. Weather is one of those things that's always on the move.

A goal realized

The rain that fell on Saturday turned the world into ice on Sunday. The streets and the rooftops were white. If you took a picture of it, it would look like snow. But if you touched it, you could see that it was really tiny pebbles of ice.

This was the kind of morning when most people figure the best thing to do is stay inside. But not us.

After my father lost his job, Sundays changed around our house. Among other things, the whole family started going to church every week.

"I can sleep late any day of the week now," he explained. "It doesn't have to be Sunday."

"But what about the people who have to go to school?" I asked. "When do they get a day off?"

"I can't help that," he said.

My father, my mother, my sister, my grandmother, and I all sat together. With the girls' purses and everybody's coats, we took up an entire pew. We stood up to sing songs. We sat down to listen to words. We also sat down to listen to the choir sing and to pass the offering plate, which went all the way down our row with only my grandmother kicking in.

The minister talked for a long time about achieving your goals in life, a subject he said was timely because this was Super Bowl Sunday, something I had not realized, since I am one of the few kids at school who does not keep up with football. I prefer shooting baskets and thinking about things.

After church I hung out with Orwell and listened to the sound of ice being blown against the windows. It's the unique sound of crystals breaking by the thousands, the sound of frozen pieces of clouds shattering into even smaller pieces, falling into gutters, onto driveways, and into yards where the raggedy starlings are the only creatures brave enough or dumb enough or desperate enough to be out searching for food.

I was getting plenty discouraged about Orwell ever walking again. I said to him, "Listen! Hear that? That's the sound of fat chances breaking into slim chances."

But for some reason, I found myself saying a prayer for him.

That night, my father and I watched the game together. We sat in front of the big screen TV eating our dinner from plastic trays that we balanced on our laps. When we asked her very politely, my mother brought us refills.

It was about halfway into the second quarter — when Denver threw a pass over the heads of the Atlanta guys all the way to the other end of the field — when I first started putting two and two together. BRONCOS TRAMPLE FALCONS. Denver Broncos. Atlanta Falcons.

My horoscope!

Then, when I heard the guys on TV talk about how the Denver quarterback already had one Super Bowl ring and it looked like he was going to get another, all the pieces just fell into place.

BRONCOS TRAMPLE FALCONS. Then a number. Then GRAB SECOND RING. But what was the number?

"I'll be right back," I told my father.

"Get me one, too," he said.

I hurried to Orwell's hideout. Yesterday's newspaper was folded neatly beneath him.

"Excuse me, Orwell," I said. "This will just take a minute."

It wasn't the most pleasant reading I've ever done, since Orwell had been using the newspaper for more than a day, but you can forgive your friends a lot, especially when it's not their fault. Anyway, I found what I was looking for. A four-digit number: 3419.

"No way!" I said out loud. "Nobody gets that many points in a football game!"

Have you ever noticed how things that are obvious often do not start out that way? It's because you were expecting them to be something else. So you work really hard trying to figure out a problem, and just when you begin to look at it a little differently, all of a sudden your brain goes Bing! and the answer is staring you right in the face, as plain as a little brown rabbit.

The number was not 3419. It was 34 to 19. BRONCOS TRAMPLE FALCONS 34 19 GRAB SECOND RING. The Denver Broncos beat the Atlanta Falcons 34 to 19 for Denver's second straight Super Bowl victory! That's what my horoscope was trying to say!

My hands were shaking when I sat down again beside my father.

"I think I know how this game is going to end," I said. "I think Denver's going to win."

"So it would appear," my father agreed. "So it would appear."

A tousle-haired boy

On Groundhog Day the weather turned bitterly cold and stayed that way for a week. Even the most determined groundhog dared not venture out for long.

Slowly, the unusually severe freeze crept deeper and deeper into the ground. The backyard goldfish pond, a little four-by-six-foot oval dug two feet deep and lined with black plastic, froze into a solid block of ice. Eleven black and orange goldfish, ranging from a few inches in length to two monsters each more than a foot long, were displayed beneath the surface in suspended animation, locked solidly in the ice in mid-swim, their fins extended, their mouths open in astonished mid-gulp. Further down I could see the lifeless bodies of two unlucky leopard frogs. I suspected there might be more of them dug into the mud.

I pounded on the glassy surface with a shovel. It bounced back into the air like a basketball. There was no hope for these water dwellers. Their luck had definitely run out.

Why does it happen like this? I wondered. Why

must creatures, through no fault of their own, be run over or frozen solid? I couldn't figure it out. Some detective!

The Super Bowl score turned out just exactly as my horoscope had predicted. At first, I kept the information under my hat, as I had been advised. At one point, I made a stab at mentioning it to my father, but since my mother had disposed of the stinky newspaper that contained the proof, he wasn't buying it.

"Of course the final score was in the paper," he said. "The Super Bowl is one of the biggest shows on TV. The newspaper has to report the results."

"But this was before the game!" I insisted.

"That's impossible," he replied.

"Well, it's interesting you should say that," I responded, "because look at what my horoscope — our horoscope — says for today!"

I thrust the comics page of the newspaper into his hands. I had just finished deciphering Scorpio's message. It said

THINGS ONLY SEEM IMPOSSIBLE BEFORE THEY HAPPEN.

My father took a moment to decode the seven special numbers, then announced, "There's a reason they put this stuff in with the funnies, you know."

What I didn't tell my father was that this latest horoscope was an installment in yet another series, this time apparently having to do with life's tougher questions. Over the past week, I had received

THE MEANING OF LIFE IS TO SEE

LEARN BY DOING THERE'S NO OTHER WAY

UNDERSTAND YOURSELF AND
YOU WILL UNDERSTAND EVERYTHING

WHAT YOU CHOOSE TO DO TODAY MATTERS
and
BE WHO YOU REALLY ARE ALL DAY.

This last astrological suggestion had been very helpful at school. In fact, in science class, when I held up my hand to answer a question, I blabbed on about what was happening to the wild animals that live around here, even though it had little to do with the original question. Afterward, this one boy came up to me in the hall and said, "I liked what you said to the teacher. I don't know if he got it, but I did."

He had brown hair that looked like his mother had mussed it with her hands as he left for school. The rest of the school day was great.

Naturally, I told Orwell all about it. He was very attentive. Most people would look at Orwell and think he was just sitting there bored. But I knew him pretty well by now. Orwell was always thinking. He looks like he's not moving, but inside his little brain, where he doesn't need to use his feet, ideas are hopping around like popcorn in a pan.

A brainstorm

My father's job during this troublesome time in our lives consisted primarily of buying lottery tickets. Sometimes I would accompany him on the two-minute road trip to the Saturn-Mart at the corner of our winding street and the busy four-lane boulevard that leads commuters to and from the highway.

There are a dozen different kinds of lottery tickets for sale at the Saturn-Mart, each promising a chance on a fortune for as little as a dollar. My father never spends more than two dollars at a time.

"You only need one set of numbers to win," he said.

"Then why buy two?" I asked.

"Just in case," he replied.

A two-dollar ticket gets you two rows of six numbers each. One of the numbers is more valuable than the other five. If you get all the numbers right, you win millions. If you get five of them, but miss the most valuable one, you still win thousands.

Once in a while, there's a picture in the newspaper of some guy winning a bundle. He's always somebody you never heard of.

Meanwhile, my horoscopes had switched into a

more personal mode. One sunny morning, I was greeted with this insight:

YOUR SISTER WANTS YOU FOR A FRIEND.

The next day, Scorpio was advised

YOUR MOTHER NEEDS HELP AROUND THE HOUSE.

Each time, I did as I was told. My sister and my mother were so grateful for my small acts of kindness that I figured it wouldn't hurt to be nicer to them all the time.

On the day I accompanied my father to the Saturn-Mart, my horoscope gave me an especially handy tip:

STUDY SCHOOL BOOKS TONIGHT
POP QUIZ TOMORROW.

As my father was paying for his two-dollar ticket to easy street, I had a low-level brainstorm.

"How much does a newspaper cost?" I asked.

"Fifty cents," the clerk said.

"I'll take one," I told him.

"Why waste your money?" my father asked as he wasted two perfectly good dollars. "That's exactly like the one we have at home."

"Maybe," I replied mysteriously. "And maybe not."

Orwell offers a clue

Tap-tap-tap-ta-tap!

The cat was waiting outside Orwell's door when I arrived and announced myself with our secret knock.

"Scram!" I told him, giving the sly feline a gentle shove with my sock-covered toes. "*Sortez!*"

"Take a look at this, Orwell," I blurted out the moment I entered his peaceful hideout. "Same newspaper. Same day. Same astrological sign. Different horoscope. What do you make of it?"

The newspaper I'd plucked from the curb in front of my house carried the half-light, half-dark moon-that-can't-make-up-its-mind sign and warned me of an impending challenge at school:

STUDY SCHOOL BOOKS TONIGHT
POP QUIZ TOMORROW.

But under the identical neutral moon in the newspaper I'd picked up at the Saturn-Mart, Scorpio's daily prediction was

STAY ON TOP OF WHAT IS HAPPENING.

"I suppose they could both mean the same thing," I admitted. "But the one in the home-delivered newspaper is much more specific. I mean, under the circumstances, you'd have to be a complete idiot not to do exactly what it says."

Dutifully, I opened my math book and turned to the appropriate chapter. Orwell stared pleasantly at me, twitching his nose.

"Not that I really believe it," I added. "But, you know, just in case."

Orwell craned his neck and yawned. His tiny pink tongue extended slightly as he stretched his upper body. He seemed bored.

"I wonder how they do it," I said.

Orwell stretched his forelegs until his paws touched the curled-up edge of the newspaper that lined his bathtub bed. He casually raised his right paw above the paper's brittle edge. With those cushioned, circular pads that protect his furry feet from cold and shock, he softly sounded out a signal.

Tap-tap-tap-ta-tap, went Orwell's little rabbit foot. *Tap-tap-tap-ta-tap!*

A taste of spring

It was one of those late winter days where you'd swear it was spring. The sun was shining and a warm breeze had brought with it the aroma of a distant rain that never arrived.

It was a great day to be alive and kicking. It was a

great day to be outside.

Strapped securely into my sister's pink umbrella-style doll stroller, Orwell watched the world go by as if he didn't have a single care in it. Trotting along beside us, sniffing excitedly, first at Orwell, then the trees, then the edges of the sidewalk, was the elderly family dog, hardly believing his good fortune at being freed from the dull routine of the house.

Our little parade must have made an amusing sight, but I didn't care what passing strangers might think. I was following the instructions of my horoscope for this fine day in February and I felt like a million dollars.

The morning after Orwell surprised me with his mastery of our secret knock, the message that appeared in my horoscope was

IT'S NOT WITH THE TONGUE WE SPEAK.

You did not have to be a great detective to see that my messages were somehow being customized for my eyes alone. So when the next day's home-thrown horoscope suggested beneath a familiar smile face moon

WHY NOT TAKE YOU-KNOW-WHO FOR A WALK,

I responded by saying, "Why not indeed!"

What a sight we were! We ambled, we trotted, we

strolled. The three of us paraded merrily through the neighborhood, walking all the way to the baseball fields behind the junior college before we even thought of turning around.

We saw birds and squirrels and a big, brown woodchuck waddling near his burrow in a field. A flock of geese heading north crossed over our heads making sounds like the squeeze bulb horn on my sister's bicycle. Gray and white clouds boiled up from the flat prairie like great mountains in the sky. When we finally got home, the poor old dog collapsed on his bed behind the sofa and snored for hours.

I returned Orwell to his hideout, but I did not return the doll stroller to my sister.

"You're really something, Orwell," I said to him admiringly.

Like Punxsutawney Phil, Groundhog Day's famous weather-predicting rodent, it seemed that Orwell also had a gift, a knack for brightening up the day.

Noises in the night

The next afternoon, when I got home from school, my mother was fussing at my father.

"We are not going to wait until we get calls from the neighbors. We are going to deal with it now," she was saying to him. "It stinks."

By "we" she meant him and me, and it soon

45

became clear that by "it" she meant the backyard pond. And you may think that you know what "stink" means, but unless you have had your hands in a dank blackwater coffin like my father and I encountered that balmy afternoon, you do not have any idea what stink really means.

The change in the weather had melted the ice and freed the goldfish from their icy prison. They floated upside down on the surface of the water, stiff, swollen, and pale. Even worse were the dim, white shapes of leopard frogs drifting like ghostly blimps halfway to the bottom.

It was like the part in horror movies on TV where you hide your face behind your open fingers, peeking only to find out if it's over.

This one wasn't going to be over until my father and I had scooped out every last cold-blooded, foul-smelling soul. We used a fishing net, trying not to touch the bodies. I dug a grave in my mother's garden. The mud clung to my shoes and got on my hands.

Again and again, we turned the net upside down, plopping the victims one on top of the other. Using a circulating pump that had been purchased to create a waterfall, we attached a long black tube and drained the pond. A terrible smell spread across our yard.

Inside the house, the telephone rang and rang again. Wisely, I thought, my mother did not answer.

That night I woke several times from restless

dreams, worried about Orwell. Once, shortly after four, as I lay face up on the pillow, frightened of the strange, vague shapes illuminated by the lighted numbers on my clock, I heard the telltale rumble of the newspaper truck. I listened to it slowing down, speeding up, and slowing down again each time it came near a subscriber's driveway. I heard the thuds and thumps and thwacks as the papers sometimes hit their concrete mark and sometimes landed in a yard. I listened and kept on listening until I heard the truck clatter around the corner. I listened even longer until I heard it drive away.

The stars speak a different language

Nothing lasts. One day you get a smile face. The next day you're staring at a frown. This hardly seems fair. If the good times are just going to kiss you and move on, what can you count on?

While shooting baskets in the driveway that afternoon, I worked on putting two and two together. The subject under cranial review, of course, was Orwell.

Right after I had asked Orwell the question about how the horoscope messages were being customized, he had given the secret knock, something he had never done before.

It was possible that Orwell had learned the secret knock by listening to me give it day after day, and, like a trained parrot, he had simply mimicked it. But my instincts told me that his response had a much bigger meaning.

I decided to confront him.

He was in his bathtub nonchalantly gnawing on the fat end of a carrot.

"I have to know," I told him. "If you're doing this, please tell me why. I'll look for your answer in tomorrow's newspaper."

Orwell rotated his ears in my direction, then alternately moved them back and forth, like upside-down legs walking through the air. I took this to mean, "OK."

The next morning I was up before sunrise and out on the lawn. In the hazy yellow light provided by the distant streetlamp, I opened the paper and flipped the pages toward the back, where the comics are. One by one I found the words for Scorpio. "Je" was the first word. *Probably initials,* I thought. Then came "vous." *Wait a minute,* I thought, *that's a French word*. It means "you." The next word was "explique." That was French, too, but I didn't know what it meant. Then, "pour" "que" "vous" "compreniez." The message was

JE VOUS EXPLIQUE POUR QUE VOUS COMPRENIEZ.

Holy smokes! I thought. *What's going on here?* My entire horoscope was in French and I couldn't translate it!

"ORWELL!" I shouted. "WHY ARE YOU DOING THIS?"

Suddenly, up and down the street as far as I could see, light streamed out through bedroom windows as if connected by a single strand. Dogs began barking. Doors slammed. Across the street, a small child cried out for its mother, while its father called out to me, "PIPE DOWN!"

Ooops.

Thanks to a mysterious little bilingual rabbit, I had inadvertently awakened the whole neighborhood.

Suspicions confirmed

My school smells like broccoli cooking. The aroma hits you the moment you step inside. It's not exactly a bad smell, but if you were choosing smells to surround yourself with, it's not one you'd pick, either.

My school has smelled like this for a long time. I noticed it the first minute of the first day I set foot in the place. That afternoon, when my mother asked me, "How was school?" I told her that it was too big, lasted too long, and smelled like broccoli cooking.

"Oh, all junior high schools smell like that," she said. "Just wait until you get to high school! It smells like cauliflower!"

My French teacher is not really a French teacher.

She's really somebody's mother who volunteered to offer French instruction for a half-hour before the last bell two days a week. So I had to wait nearly all day inside that vegetable steamer that's my home away from home to get my horoscope message translated.

"Let me see," the French-speaking mother said, examining the phrase I had carefully copied from the newspaper. "*'Je vous explique pour que vous compreniez.'* Why, this is an exercise from next week's lesson. It means, 'I am explaining to you so you will understand.'"

Orwell! No doubt about it!

People always say a kid's life is easy. But I'm not so sure. What with teachers, parents, preachers, and now, it appeared, a rabbit hiding behind my horoscope like the great Oz behind the curtain, I had no shortage of people — and creatures — telling me what to do.

A plan gone wrong

The first time Orwell sent me a message that might have made me rich, I had kept it to myself. The second time he did it, I nearly got him killed.

TRY FOUR NINETEEN TWENTY-ONE
TWENTY-TWO TWENTY-SEVEN TWELVE.

This is what my prophetic rabbit advised in my daily horoscope one bright February morning. Unlike the cryptic scores he'd sent me for the Super Bowl, I figured out this combination right away.

The lottery!

You'd think this one would have been a slam dunk. Something even a sixth-grader could have done. You know the number. You buy the ticket. You win the money. *Bingo!* You're rich and all your troubles are behind you. But maybe Orwell had something else up his sleeve.

I strapped Orwell into his stroller and the two of us set out for the Saturn-Mart as soon as school was out. In my pocket I carried a crisp dollar bill. The distance to my destination was little more than a mile, but as it turned out, I might as well have tried to travel to the moon.

It was, as I have said, a sunny day, and since the chilly morning, it had warmed up another twenty degrees or so, bringing out native and domesticated animals of every description.

Squirrels bounced across lawns, trying to recall last fall's hiding places. Geese descended from the skies to a sudden graceless landing on a nearby lake. Dogs paced behind fences like tigers in a zoo. A hidden, natural orchestra of caws and twitters and tweets accompanied my rabbit and me on fortune's journey down the sidewalk. Only the people, it seemed, chose to remain huddled indoors.

I was giddy with excitement. I was off to see the wizard! Or, more accurately, I had the wizard with me and was off to claim the loot. Whichever it was, it made me careless, and fortune does not favor the careless.

The first thing that happened was that I slid in some goose poop on the sidewalk. I am no expert in goose poop, but I can testify that it is extremely slippery stuff. As my feet flew out from under me, I grasped, as any falling person would do, for something to keep me aright. All that lay within my reach, of course, was Orwell's — formerly my sister's — stroller, but its fragile aluminum frame was meant to support a plastic doll, not a nearly grown rabbit and a full-size, crashing girl. As my feet flew up, so did it, and as it flew, so, too, did Orwell, his little plastic seat belt no more help than Scotch tape would have been.

I landed on the concrete, scraping my elbow and my knee. The crippled Orwell tumbled onto the grass, where, if events had somehow at that moment ceased, all might yet have been well.

But, no, one thing always leads to another.

I had seen the geese when they arrived. I had heard the dogs bark as we passed by. Nevertheless, when the big red Irish setter dashed across the lawn and scooped up Orwell into his drooling mouth, I was unprepared to act. Preoccupied with my injured joints that by now were seeping blood and sending sharp signals of pain to my inadequate brain, I hadn't even time to rise to my feet before the copper-colored kidnapper was well out of sight.

"ORWELL!" I screamed, hobbling in the direction that the rabbit and the dog had gone. "Orwell, come back!"

Dogs are furtive creatures, more cautious than they are smart. If you give a dog a bone, he will take it a short distance away, where he thinks he is unseen, before beginning his methodical devouring of the prize. It was this dumb dog instinct, not my swift action, that spared Orwell's life this day.

I found the stupid setter sprawled behind a bush just around the corner of a house. As I burst into view breathing hard and breathing fire, he looked up with disappointment in his eyes, knowing that for now the jig was up.

"Drop him!" I commanded. "Or you die!"

The Orwell that I retrieved was a slobbery wet rag of a rabbit. His fur was matted. His ears stuck out in two directions. His heart was racing like a go-cart on a track. But, thankfully, nothing about his appearance indicated that he'd become an appetizer.

I felt as bad as it is possible for a kid to feel. This little rabbit trusted me with his life and I had let him down.

"C'mon, Orwell," I said glumly. "It's getting dark. Let's go home."

My mother cleaned my wounds, wrapped a big

white bandage around my elbow, and put a patch on my knee. My father helped me dry Orwell and return him to his tub. That night, Orwell didn't touch his supper.

When my father asked me how it happened, I told him we had been on our way to buy a lottery ticket. I told him I'd had a hunch about the numbers that would win. I told him I was sure I was right.

"Oh, didn't you know?" he said. "Kids can't buy lottery tickets. It's gambling. For kids, gambling is against the law."

Orwell stops publishing

In a previous communication, my rabbit had advised

LEARN BY DOING THERE'S NO OTHER WAY.

According to Orwell, our mistakes are simply the price we must pay for our education.

But what a price it is! To learn to watch out for goose poop on the sidewalk cost me a whopping twenty-four million dollars! That's how much the winning lottery ticket would have paid, if anybody had held the winning lottery ticket, which, according to the next day's newspaper, they did not.

I could have been that winner.

Just as I'd expected, the numbers that Orwell sent me through my horoscope that morning were the very numbers that were drawn by lottery officials that evening. I shall never forget them. Four. Nineteen. Twenty-one. Twenty-two. Twenty-seven. And twelve. These numbers will follow me for the rest of my days.

And to think, I came that close! What rotten luck!

I suspected that Orwell shared this view. Bearing an inconclusive half-light, half-dark moon, his latest message to me read

LUCK MARKET IS CLOSED

TRY AGAIN LATER.

The rabbit, it seemed, had had enough for now.

I tried to get my poor overwrought brain to change the channel. That's when I remembered that Valentine's Day was coming up soon.

Valentine's Day is a holiday whose purpose, like so many things, remains a mystery to me. At my old school, the kids all exchanged little printed messages of affection, usually with cartoons on them and frequently in rhyme, heartfelt stuff that they bought by the bagful. At my new school, it seems, it's more important to be cool. I was halfway thinking of giving a valentine to the tousle-haired boy who had spoken to me after class, but what if the entire episode turned out like the lottery?

How much disappointment can one kid stand?

There was no point in asking Orwell for advice. Clearly, he was off duty. I decided to ask my parents instead.

"Think low-key," my mother suggested after a moment of thought. "Seventh grade is an awkward time in a boy's life. He probably wants to be noticed, but he may not appreciate being noticed being noticed."

"Huh?" I said.

"Give him a valentine, but don't do it in front of other people," she explained.

"And make sure it's not too fancy," my father chimed in. "You've got to have deniability."

"Deniability?"

"You have to be able to claim that what you gave him was the same as you gave everybody else, even if you didn't give anybody else anything at all. Just in case what you gave him doesn't go over."

"Just in case," I repeated, nodding my head as if I understood.

And to think they call this a holiday!

My comic valentine

No sailor would attempt to cross the sea without a compass. No farmer would plant his seeds without first consulting his almanac. No weatherman would set foot outside his door without consulting his gauges. But with Orwell off his feed, my horoscope messages were completely blank. I had entered the dark ages, condemned to face each day without a clue.

People say that life has its ups and downs, a popular point of view implying that if you just wait, bad luck, like bad weather, will eventually turn to good. But there's another less common homily that can also apply to fortune's erratic direction, namely, that things will go from bad to worse before the cycle repeats itself.

Outside my school are soccer fields that stretch from the parking lot to the subdivisions in the distance. Flat, treeless, and close-cropped like a lawn, the soccer fields are of little use for anything but band practice and that single, frantic imported sport for which they were created. No bird, no squirrel, no rabbit can inhabit this empty space.

But deep beneath the ground, under a row of bright yellow warning posts, ingenious engineers have laid a pipeline, a highway for natural gas, extending from the oil fields of Oklahoma to the car factories of Detroit. Millions of tons of volatile, explosive energy surge beneath the feet of children at play, and no one's worried. No one, that is, but me. I think about it every time I stand there.

I think that I am standing on a bomb.

This is where I was standing and what I was thinking when I handed the handmade valentine to the tousle-haired boy from class.

"Here," I mumbled. "This one's yours."

"For me? Thank you," he responded as he climbed into a minivan waiting at the curb.

I had constructed it the night before using a pale yellow notebook divider and a page from a glossy magazine. Cut into a traditional heart shape, it showed a hilly countryside in full bloom, with a thatched-roof cottage in the distance and a young girl picking flowers in the foreground. At the last minute, I had decided to write the message in French, thinking this would make the valentine both more special and, to the casual uninvited eye, more private. "*Les enfants aiment se moquer d'un singe,*" I had penned in purple marker across the top, intending to say, "Kids like you are a world of fun." My hope was that he would think the same about me.

Fate would have been kinder to me if, at that moment, it had blown up the pipeline in a boiling ball of flame. The phrase that I had so hastily and ineptly assembled from the worksheets in my notebook did not say what I thought. As I was to learn to my profound dismay in French class the following day, what I had expressed so earnestly to the tousle-haired boy was, "Children like to make fun of a monkey."

I went home to my silent rabbit in shame.

The science of dreams

Forget being a private detective! I decided. Forget weather! Forget basketball and trombone playing and veterinary medicine! I was now interested only in the world of dreams, in the science of them, in discovering how they work.

There are principles that apply to motion and matter in dreams, just as there are scientific laws that rule our waking lives. The only problem is that with dreams, no one has ever figured out these principles.

With ordinary earth physics, if you step from the edge of a cliff, you fall and hit the rocks below. Nine times out of ten, you're history. But in dreams, if you step out into space, you never die. You're always transported safely to someplace else. No matter how many times you dream of stepping off the edge, you're always saved. This is dream physics at its finest.

In my dreams, my mother and my father do not fight, my father has a job that he enjoys, the tousle-haired boy at school is my friend, and Orwell can hop like other rabbits.

For a while my favorite place to be was in bed. I went to school, of course, and fulfilled my obligation to care for Orwell and the family dog. But I did little else but lie upon my pillow and think about the science that applies to dreams.

I wondered if there might not be some project I could do for the science fair this year. Some dream experiment. I knew from all my hours of thinking that thoughts can stick to things. A dream fact that was forgotten when you stepped into the bathroom suddenly comes back when you return to bed. That's because thoughts swirl around like smoke. They attach to objects, like smudges, like grime, like dust, and thus, on contact, this memory dust can be stirred back into consciousness, or something close, before it goes away.

This was my theory. My hypothesis was that if you changed your pillow, you would change the content of your dreams. Old pillow, old dreams. New pillow, new dreams. A brand-new pillow would work to clean the windows of the mind, making dreams fresher, more vivid, clearer. A new pillow, I conjectured, would be a fresh start for the subconscious. And did I ever wish for a fresh start!

Everything that happens in our lives is connected to everything else. It's all strung together end to end. First this, then that. Fetch the newspaper, find the rabbit. Find the rabbit, receive the messages. Receive the messages, then what?

I didn't know.

But messing up on the lottery and the valentine put me in bed thinking about dream science, and that, in turn, got me to wishing I had a new pillow, and the act of asking my mother to get me a new pillow caused the next thing to happen.

Who can say if it was luck or fate?

Who really knows the difference?

Animal magnetism

My grandmother is as healthy as a horse. Even so, once a week she goes to the doctor, just as once a week she goes to the hairdresser and once a week she attends the sale at the department store at the mall.

Shopping for bargains and getting her hair done and going to the doctor are weekly rituals that are as important to my grandmother as going to church is for some people. Without these routines to get her out of her maintenance-provided condominium, my grandmother would be as much of a shut-in as my paraplegic rabbit.

Years of specializing in being a patient, a department store customer, and a beauty salon regular have produced some interesting results, some obvious, some less so.

The most conspicuous result of my grandmother's routine is her hair. It doesn't look like real hair at all. It is thin, stiff, and slightly pink, more like cotton candy than human hair. When the wind blows, it does not. When it rains, she becomes anxious and wraps her head in a plastic bag.

Less obvious than her unusual hair, but also a crown of sorts, is my grandmother's great status at her doctor's office, where she ranks among this businessman's most valuable customers. All he is required to do for my grandmother is keep a few current magazines in his waiting room, ask her about her two grandchildren, and give her some pills to take home.

Finally, my grandmother's limited but repetitive activity has given her an incredible knowledge of manufactured goods. If it is for sale in a department store, she knows everything there is to know about it.

So it was only logical that when I asked my mother for a new pillow, she, in turn, being conscious of expenses now that my father was unemployed, asked her mother for advice on what kind of pillow to get.

Naturally, my grandmother wanted to know why I needed a new pillow and why her firstborn grandchild was spending so much time in bed. After a long and increasingly tense conversation with my mother, my grandmother concluded, somewhat erroneously, that I was merely moping over the condition of my run-over rabbit.

"But what else can I do?" my mother lamented to the woman who had raised her almost single-handedly from the moment she was born.

"Simple," my grandmother, the fountain of child-rearing wisdom, snapped back. "Fix the rabbit and you fix the girl."

And this is how I wound up one day after school waiting with Orwell to get an MRI.

MRI stands for magnetic resonance imaging. It used to be called nuclear magnetic resonance imaging but the "nuclear" part scared everybody so they changed it. What MRI is, is a way of taking pictures inside your body using a giant magnet and radio waves. The pictures that you get are better than X-rays.

Getting these pictures, however, is a lot more complicated than X-rays, and the more complicated something is, the more expensive it is. That's why most people just get X-rays even though the pictures are not very good. That's why Orwell just got X-rays even though when the veterinarian looked at them he couldn't see what was wrong.

Fortunately for Orwell, he was now associated with me, and I was associated with my grandmother, who had connections with a successful doctor who had invested in an MRI facility right across the street from his office where my grandmother hung out every Thursday morning, rain or shine, plastic bag or no plastic bag.

"We sometimes get people with teddy bears," the technician said, ushering me into what looked like a storage room for big metal parts. "But we've never had anybody with a rabbit before."

"His name is Orwell," I explained.

"I hope he's not claustrophobic," the technician said.

"Why do you ask?" I replied.

The place was beginning to remind me of my one and only trip to the emergency room, when I had gotten a raisin stuck up my nose. I was a lot younger, of course.

"We have to put you in there and it takes a while," the technician explained.

"In there" turned out to be a metal tunnel as big as a Volkswagen. "A while," I was soon to learn, meant forty-five minutes. And "you" did not simply mean the injured Orwell, it meant me holding the injured Orwell.

Nobody had mentioned this part to me.

"You have to keep him very still or the pictures won't be any good," the technician said.

It's noisy inside an MRI machine. It clatters and bangs and burps. When it's doing what it is supposed to do, it sounds just like it's broken. And when it stops, and you think it's over and you're going to be freed, it starts right up again.

Like luck stuck on going from bad to worse, the cycle keeps repeating.

Despite the noise, or possibly because of it, Orwell snuggled down into the cavity in my chest, like a rabbit in a grassy nest in a meadow, and went to sleep.

The Year of the Rabbit

"Rabbits are not put together especially well," the new veterinarian said. "They have very weak backs." A younger man than I'd expected, he had thick, dark hair, a bright smile, and a surprisingly clean-smelling office.

When my grandmother and I had first arrived, there were no other patients in his waiting room. A receptionist not much older than I am, with short red hair and a round red face, had given my grandmother a form to fill out while I looked around the room.

The waiting room was about as big as our family room, but much tidier and more restful-looking, with green upholstered chairs, green-striped wallpaper, and green and tan carpet with no visible stains. On the walls hung two nearly identical watercolors of a country garden in full summer bloom. Beneath them, three brass lamps glowed on dark wood tables. At one end of the room, a people-sized wheelchair was folded up against the wall.

"That's for some of our patients' owners," the receptionist explained when she saw me staring. "They're not all as young as you."

The new veterinarian greeted us warmly. He gently lifted Orwell from the plastic travel cage I'd borrowed from my sister's cat, scratching the rabbit's knobby head, just like I do.

"With such weak backs, hind limb paralysis is fairly common among rabbits," he continued. "Many times, it's environmental. Toxins in their food and water. Viruses. That sort of thing. But we see a lot of trauma, too."

"Orwell got hit by a truck," I explained. "At least, that's what I think happened."

I handed him a brown envelope that was as big as a briefcase. It was labeled MRI FILM PLEASE DO NOT BEND. Inside were six sheets of black film, each about the size of the poster board you'd use to make a science fair display. On each sheet were fifteen different negative images of Orwell's insides. One by one, the new veterinarian held the pictures up to the light.

"The MRI is the single greatest advance in medical diagnostics," he remarked appreciatively. "You can get a 3-D picture of anything!"

"Can you see what's wrong with Orwell?" I asked.

"It looks like there's been a shifting of the vertebra," he said. "See here, where it narrows?" He pointed to a picture on the sheet in his hand, but I couldn't tell exactly what on the picture he was pointing at. "It didn't show up on the X-rays because the muscles had put the vertebra back together. Unfortunately, they didn't do it well enough. The spinal cord is inflamed."

"What can we do?" I asked him.

"We can take the pressure off and we can pin it back together," he said.

"And that will work?" I asked.

"If we're lucky," he replied. "It all depends on how much damage has been done to his spinal cord."

On the way back home, my grandmother stopped to pick up supper for the family at the Imperial Garden. I went in with her while Orwell waited in the car.

Even though everything on the menu at the Imperial Garden has different names, when it is served, it is all pretty much the same food. That's why I always get sweet and sour pork. It's a little different from the rest of the food. It is oranger and it is sweeter.

While we were waiting for the food to be prepared, I noticed a poster announcing a party in celebration of Chinese New Year. It said that the new year was called the Year of the Rabbit.

"Wow! But I thought New Year's Day had already come and gone!" I blurted out.

"There is always more than one way of looking at things," the proprietor explained. "Instead of the sun, the Chinese calendar goes by the cycles of the moon. The Chinese lunar zodiac is inhabited by twelve animals, each with its own characteristics. Each year is given a name of one of those animals."

He handed me a place mat from an unoccupied table. It had pictures of all the different animals. In addition to a rabbit, there was a tiger, an ox, a rat, a boar, a dog, a rooster, a monkey, a sheep, a horse, a snake, and a dragon. Listed beside these animals were their special years and the effect they were supposed to have on those years.

The place mat explained that because the rabbit is such a gentle animal, the Year of the Rabbit would be one that is peaceful and prosperous. Of all the signs to be born under, the place mat said, the rabbit is the happiest. That's when I saw that not only was the new year the Year of the Rabbit, but the last Year of the Rabbit was the year that I was born.

"Now isn't that a coincidence," I said. "Wait until I tell Orwell!"

That night after polishing off the rice that was left in the square white cartons that pile up like autumn leaves after an Imperial Garden meal, I shot the breeze with my ailing little friend. His operation was scheduled for the following week and I didn't want him to worry.

"Why is it, Orwell," I mused, "that nearly every single day has some sort of special designation? Take this month, for instance. Already we've had Groundhog Day, Valentine's Day, Presidents' Day, Chinese New Year, Ash Wednesday, and so many anniversaries of important historical events that even my teachers can't keep them straight. It's like there's no room for something brand new to happen, such as Rabbit Surgery Day, for instance, because we're too busy commemorating all the stuff that has happened before!"

For the first time in recent days, Orwell seemed interested in what I had to say, so I continued.

"You know what I wish? I wish there were a month that had only regular days in it. No holidays. No anniversaries. Nothing requiring the purchase of a card or a gift or the singing of memorized songs. Just plain days where all anybody is expected to do is appreciate the day simply for itself. A month filled with perfectly ordinary days!"

Orwell switched his ears back and forth.

"That would be special!" I said.

A concert for Orwell

Orwell resumed publishing with these words:

BETWEEN RABBIT AND GIRL
LITTLE DIFFERENCE EXISTS.

As I got dressed for church, I "hmmmed" my customary quizzical response and bounced the thought to the back of my brain like a basketball ricocheting off a backboard.

My church is mostly shades of brown. Even so, the parts and pieces do not match. The walls are made of painted concrete blocks whose chestnut color subtly clashes with the cream brown tiles on the floor. All the woods are different, too. The beams and trusses come from evergreens, I think, while the cross is made of walnut. A member of the congregation who's a cabinetmaker crafted the pulpit and the lectern out of birch. The four long rows of wood-stained pews, purchased from another church, were once oak trees in a distant forest.

As churches go, this one is new, founded in that rabbity year when I was born, but the music that we sing goes back three or four hundred years and the words that we call Scripture go back thousands.

Many times when I sit in church I wish that I were someplace else. Playing basketball. Taking a walk. Working on a project at home. This Sunday, however, I found it restful to sit and think while the words and the music from the front of the room washed over me like waves making their offering to the beach.

What I was thinking about was the mystery of Orwell. *Why had he come? What was the source of his magic? What did he want me to do?* The answers seemed far beyond the reach of my detective skills.

And with his operation just around the corner, I was worried, too, about Orwell making it.

This Sunday the minister didn't talk about sports. Instead, his subject was healing.

"For most of what ails us," he announced with great authority in his clear, deep voice, "the best medicine is a dose of love. And if that doesn't work, double the dose!"

I didn't know what else I could do to show my love for Orwell. Already, he had more food than he could eat. His hideout was as nice a place as any rabbit could reasonably expect. Taking him outside again didn't seem like such a good idea. With my grandmother's help, he was going to have a chance at walking, although that chance could turn out to be like your chances for winning the lottery. What could I do that I wasn't already doing?

Somehow Orwell knew of my concerns, for in my horoscope the next day, I deciphered these words:

> LOVING ACTIONS MUST START
> WITH LOVING THOUGHTS.

When I did my homework in his room that night, I told Orwell that even though I hadn't figured out exactly what was going on, I was glad that I was the one who'd found him and not someone else.

Orwell replied in the morning with this:

> THE GREATEST GIFT WE GIVE IS OURSELVES.

This news made me feel closer to Orwell than ever. That's when I came up with an idea for what to do for him before his operation.

Announcing myself that night with our secret *tap-tap-tap-ta-tap*, I entered Orwell's room carrying a hard black case that when stood on its end came all the way up to my chin. The instrument inside, made of polished brass and shiny chrome, was in three pieces, each nestled in a fitted velvet valley.

I removed the short mouthpiece, the long slide section, and the bell section, whose flashy end was as big as a dinner plate. As the rabbit watched me from the tub, I put the pieces together and stood before him bearing the grand and unmistakable shape of the most-prized instrument of every band.

"*Ta-da!*" I said to Orwell, presenting my trombone.

He responded, *Tap-tap-tap-ta-tap!*

Carefully, lest the strange new sound disturb his sensitive rabbit ears, I put my lips together and pushed out a single note, a brief musical belch, to introduce the trombone's throaty tone. As I had hoped, his eyes expressed not fear, but interest.

The only piece I knew by heart was "Twinkle, Twinkle, Little Star." It seemed appropriate since I considered naming him Star so many weeks before. At any rate, it would have to do.

Without further delay, I began the concert for

Orwell.

Some people think that you just blow on a trombone and music comes out the other end. Not so.

The music must first be created by your lips. The trombone amplifies and modifies the sound, just as a hammer amplifies and directs the blows your arm delivers. It is truly all in the lips.

When I press my lips tightly together and blow with a sort of buzzing sound as hard as I can, the sound that I produce is high in pitch. When I relax my lips just slightly, and reduce the effort with which I blow, the sound is lower. I use the slide on the trombone to form each sound into just the note I want.

There are seven slide positions on the trombone. My arms are only able to reach numbers one through six, with the sixth position, where my arm is stretched as far as it can go, producing the lowest notes I can command.

There are a couple of places in "Twinkle, Twinkle, Little Star" requiring the sixth position, so I had to slow down when I came to those notes, but except for this understandable and, I think, minor flaw, I played the tune quite well — so well, in fact, that I performed it that night for Orwell many times.

Twinkle, twinkle, little star. The slide-controlled sound of fine-tuned brass plumbing bounced against the hard ceramic backboard of Orwell's tub and tile.

How I wonder what you are.

Orwell speaks

A false spring had accidentally summoned the cro-
cuses. The eager little showoffs popped up weeks
ahead of schedule. In the distance, above the rumble
of cars and trucks thundering down the expressway,
rose the twittering of hundreds of birds foolishly cel-
ebrating what they thought was the passing of winter.

From the elevation of the porch I surveyed the
lawn, looking for that familiar white bundle that
holds the news. This was the day of Orwell's operation. If ever a horoscope mattered, it was now.

I saw a paper in my next-door neighbor's driveway,
and another in the driveway after that, and still more
farther down the street. I saw one lying in the yard
across the street and another at the house next door
to it. But I did not see a paper in my yard.

I searched behind the tree and underneath the car.
I looked in the bushes and even on the roof.

There was no paper. It had not been delivered to
my house.

"Rats!" I said. "*C'est dommage!*"

With my father working on the house and my
grandmother attending the sale at the department
store at the mall, it was my mother who drove
Orwell and me to the new veterinarian's office. She

provided the alarming explanation en route.

"Your father has canceled the newspaper," she said, waiting for the light to change at an intersection as wide as a river. "He's trying to save us money."

"But I depend on the paper!" I cried.

"There's always the TV," she suggested. "Or the radio."

"They're not the same," I said.

"Well, we're all having to make sacrifices right now."

I did not wish to argue with my mother, but my father's frugal decision didn't make sense. The savings from canceling the paper couldn't be more than a few dollars. The information it had been bringing me was priceless.

At the corner of the vast and crowded intersection was an apartment complex whose big brick buildings stood in rows like brass bands in a parade. As my eyes automatically searched for something interesting to help them pass the time, they landed on what appeared to be an inverted mop in motion, a vaguely familiar object that I was startled to realize was the tousle-headed boy himself, leaving an apartment!

He was dressed in blue jeans, white tennis shoes, and a pale yellow shirt that reminded me of spring flowers. His light brown hair flew wildly as he walked toward the minivan I'd seen him get into once before.

"So that's where he lives!" I said softly.

"Where who lives?" my mother asked.

"Oh, just somebody from school," I sighed, remembering how badly I'd monkeyed up my French.

"I lived in a place like that nearly my whole life," my mother said.

"You did?"

"Uh-huh. In fact, until your father and I got married, I had never lived in a real house at all," she confided.

"Oh," I said.

"My house means a lot to me," she continued. "I don't take it for granted."

"And now you've got a rabbit living in it," I said apologetically.

"Well," she smiled, "as rabbits go, he's a pretty nice one."

It's a funny thing about parents. You think you know them pretty well and then one day they let something slip and you see them in a brand-new light.

Because of school, I couldn't stay with Orwell during his operation. The new veterinarian advised against it anyway.

"We'll call you as soon as we're sure of his condition," he promised.

There was nothing left to do but hurry to school, put my brain on "worry," and offer up a prayer.

"Please, God," I said, entering the familiar broccoli-smelling building as the last bell of the morning echoed down the hall. "Please look after your rabbit. Thank you."

That day was the longest day of my life. Math class went on into infinity. In history, the teacher tediously traced the entire Lewis and Clark expedition to the edge of the American continent and back again. Even P.E., normally a welcome break for me, ran in slow motion. Basketballs thrown into the air took forever to fall into the net, like pancake crumbs drifting down through syrup.

By afternoon the false spring had faded. The wind rose. The temperature fell. And still the day crawled on.

Never have I felt so helpless.

Never have I felt so trapped.

When I finally did get home, there was still no news about Orwell. I fixed a snack and turned on the TV, but even the world's greatest mind-numbing machine failed to work on my worried brain. I couldn't stand to wait any longer. I reached for the phone, and just as I did, it rang.

"Your rabbit is a lot tougher than he looks," the new veterinarian said, although I had trouble hearing him over the pounding of my heart. "He's been through a lot these past few weeks. It took a little longer to piece him back together than I'd originally thought."

"Is he alive?" I gasped, my first exhale since picking up the phone.

"Oh, yes, but he's sleeping, of course. He did pretty well, I think, but it will take some time to know if he'll recover all his motor functions."

"You fixed his motor?"

The new veterinarian laughed. "Actually, I wish it were that simple. Your rabbit sustained a moderately severe spinal injury and that's sometimes worse than it sounds, but he's survived being reassembled, minus a faulty part or two, so that's a good sign. From here on out, it's up to him and Mother Nature."

The new veterinarian said that if Orwell didn't take a turn for the worse, he might be able to come home in a few days.

After I hung up the phone, I just stood there breathing.

"*Merci,*" I said to my grandmother and all of her connections. "*Merci,*" I said to God.

Mother Nature, it seems, has trouble making up her mind. That night it snowed. Fat, fluffy flakes drifted down from salt-shaker clouds.

My grandmother, remembering my earlier request, brought me a pillow she'd picked up on sale at the department store at the mall. It was something of a snowflake itself, big, round, and soft — almost too fat for its pillowcase. When I lay my head down on it, it wrapped itself around my ears, softening the sounds from other rooms.

Because of it, I dreamed a brand-new dream that

night. One that was rich, colorful, and strange. I dreamed that I was an explorer leading an expedition into a vast and rugged land where no English-speaking person had dared set foot before. With me were two companions, Orwell, my faithful rabbit, and the tousle-haired boy from school.

The boy served as my interpreter, since the native people we encountered spoke nothing but French and I found spoken French to be as foreign as Chinese. What we were searching for was never clear to me. Dreams have a way of keeping secrets from the dreamer. But I remember well the feelings that I felt. One of these was that I'd known the tousle-haired boy all my life.

"How can you understand what these people are saying?" I asked him.

"It helps if you let them keep talking," he replied. "Most people just interrupt."

"And what are they saying now?" I asked him.

"They say we should follow the river."

"But which way?" I asked. "This is where the river divides!"

"They say you should follow the one that lies closest to your heart," he answered.

"That's easy," I said, remembering what I'd learned in science class about the placement of the major organs. "We will take the fork on the left," I announced.

It was then that I dreamed that Orwell spoke, even

though his mouth never moved beyond an isolated twitch, and he never uttered a sound before or since. Somehow, though, I'm pretty sure, it was Orwell who pronounced these seven dream words to me that night:

"Not so fast. See it another way."

The collected works of Orwell

Habit rules when the brain does not. The next morning, I was outside in the snow searching in vain for a snow-colored newspaper when I suddenly remembered that it wasn't coming anymore. I stretched my arms, breathed in the cold, crisp, diesel-scented air and looked around again, just in case.

There were faint tracks in the shallow snow, mostly dog footprints, including one set from the fat family dog who followed me out the door, but also some that could have been squirrels and one set that I was pretty sure had been put there by a rabbit.

In the distance, I heard the slowly rising rumble of commuters launching themselves onto the expressway. From across the street came a sudden burst of shouts, followed by the drumlike banging of pots and pans.

I felt disoriented without my horoscope. I didn't know what to do with my time. Orwell was at the new veterinarian's office. And it would be an hour before any other member of my family got out of bed.

I went inside and sat down at the kitchen counter without turning on the light. The weak aroma of last night's dinner hovered around the stove. Hamburgers slightly overcooked in the cast iron skillet. Frozen French fries baked and salted on a cookie sheet. A pot of peas with butter. Lettuce and tomatoes in a blue ceramic bowl. Scents, dreams, thoughts — even words — they all try to stick around, but we ignore them, so they leave.

This gave me an idea. I retrieved my backpack from where I'd left it by the kitchen door and wrestled my green three-ring binder from the jumbled mess inside. I would write down everything the rabbit had ever told me, like a real detective, or a proper historian, would have done all along.

It took every bit of the time that fortune had allotted me that morning, but I completed my self-imposed assignment and produced a list that looked like this:

1. UNDER NEW MANAGEMENT. WATCH FOR SPECIAL INSTRUCTIONS.

2. STAY TUNED FOR AN IMPORTANT NEWS BULLETIN.

3. KEEP ALL FURTHER COMMUNICATIONS UNDER YOUR HAT.

4. BRONCOS TRAMPLE FALCONS 34–19.

GRAB SECOND RING.

5. THE MEANING OF LIFE IS TO SEE.

6. LEARN BY DOING. THERE'S NO OTHER WAY.

7. UNDERSTAND YOURSELF AND YOU WILL UNDER-
STAND EVERYTHING.

8. WHAT YOU CHOOSE TO DO TODAY MATTERS.

9. BE WHO YOU REALLY ARE ALL DAY.

10. THINGS ONLY SEEM IMPOSSIBLE BEFORE THEY
HAPPEN.

11. YOUR SISTER WANTS YOU FOR A FRIEND.

12. YOUR MOTHER NEEDS HELP AROUND THE HOUSE.

13. STUDY SCHOOL BOOKS TONIGHT. POP QUIZ
TOMORROW.

14. IT'S NOT WITH THE TONGUE WE SPEAK.

15. WHY NOT TAKE YOU-KNOW-WHO FOR A WALK?

16. *JE VOUS EXPLIQUE POUR QUE VOUS
COMPRENIEZ.*

(I AM EXPLAINING TO YOU SO YOU WILL UNDER-
STAND.)

17. TRY 4-19-21-22-27-12.

18. LUCK MARKET IS CLOSED. TRY AGAIN LATER.

19. BETWEEN RABBIT AND GIRL LITTLE DIFFERENCE
EXISTS.

20. LOVING ACTIONS MUST START WITH LOVING
THOUGHTS.

21. THE GREATEST GIFT WE GIVE IS OURSELVES.

I left out the secret knock, since it was more of a
signal than a complete message. I couldn't decide

what to do about the dream advice, though, since I couldn't be sure that the words I had dreamed actually came from Orwell. Finally, I did add the phrase, but I put an asterisk at the end of it.

22. NOT SO FAST. SEE IT ANOTHER WAY.*

Looking it over, I couldn't help but notice that there wasn't really that much to go on. There were messages that suggested that I pay attention to other messages. There were messages obviously about specific events on certain days and intended just for me. And there were messages that I supposed might be useful to any person, anytime.

As I struggled to figure out the words on this short list, I was reminded of the book we use in church, where the actual words the main person spoke are few and far between, and the majority of the book is filled up with other people trying to explain what he meant by them. Complete understanding of the Book of Orwell could be a long time coming.

Of course, that's just one way of looking at it.

Home again

While Orwell was in the hospital recovering from surgery, I called to check on him every day, once before I left for school, and again when I got home.

Every time I called, he was sleeping. But on Friday, the veterinarian said, "This rabbit is ready to be transferred to a nursing home. Does yours have room for him?"

"You bet!" I replied.

My father took me to the pet store to buy a proper rabbit cage and other supplies so that Orwell could stay in my room. Then we hurried to pick up the patient.

Orwell was waiting for us at the front desk in a white cardboard box with round holes in the sides. I wanted to give him a hug, but because of his recent surgery, I scratched his bumpy head instead.

"Am I ever glad to see you alive!" I told him.

He laid back his ears and nuzzled my hand with his weakly vibrating nose.

Safely home, I set up his cage on a LEGO table I'd placed by the windows. I lifted Orwell out of the box with both hands as the veterinarian had instructed, and set the rabbit carefully into the center of the cage on a carpet of fresh, aromatic pine shavings.

Orwell sprawled on his stomach with his tiny legs trailing behind him like the tail of a kite. He made no impression in the pine litter. The poor little guy weighed next to nothing.

Orwell was in as bad a shape as I've ever seen him, worse than the day I found him in the front yard, worse than the time he got carried off by the Irish setter. He was a limp and nearly lifeless rabbit now, a rabbit skin filled with loose and leftover parts, a beanbag toy and little more.

How much luck did he have left? I wondered.

"Can he walk yet?" My sister and her wily cat had followed me into my room.

"I don't think so," I answered. "It's not supposed to happen that fast." Then, so I didn't attract bad luck by expressing too much wishful thinking, I added, "If it ever does."

"Then why is he in a cage?" she inquired.

"I'm not sure," I replied. "Maybe it's to protect him from your cat."

"He won't hurt Orwell. He's just curious about anything new."

It was true that the cat was always the first to inspect any box or shopping bag brought into the house. No sooner would you set it on the floor than he'd sniff it, walk around it, climb into it, sit on it, and generally claim it for his own until he eventually got bored and moved on.

Now the inquisitive feline had his face up to Orwell's wire mesh door. He stared blankly at the quiet rabbit and swished his tail.

"I don't know," I said. "It looks to me like he wants to eat him."

"I don't think he could," my sister said. "They're almost the same size."

Suddenly, in a single, skillful bound, my sister's cat leapt onto the top of Orwell's cage. He stretched out

85

his full furry length, placed his head down on the wire, and studied the little rabbit from above.

Orwell seemed unperturbed.

As my sister and I continued to observe, the acrobatic cat rolled over on his side, rested his head against his forelegs and, as cats around the world are so adept at doing, promptly fell asleep.

"He doesn't look very dangerous to me," my sister said.

Soon the old dog came padding in, his belly barely clearing the carpet. Seeing the cat and the rabbit apparently enjoying an afternoon snooze, he decided to join them, collapsing like a deflated beach ball at the foot of the platform supporting Orwell's cage.

"That's strange," I said. "I thought they were natural enemies."

"People can change, you know," my sister said, an accidental insight that burst from her mouth like the burp that follows swallows of fizzy soda.

"Well, Orwell," I said, "you sure have a knack for making friends. I guess we're going to have to extend the visiting hours a little tonight."

The wheel of fortune

There is nothing unusual about the sight of FOR SALE signs in my neighborhood. People come and go

86

for many reasons. So when the school bus dropped me off one chilly afternoon and a freshly planted FOR SALE sign beckoned from the house across the street, I barely even noticed, dismissing the commonplace placard with, "*Cela m'est egal*" ("It's all the same to me").

But once I got inside, it was a different story.

"Did you hear?" my father asked. "The what's-their-names, you know, the people who live across the street? They won the lottery yesterday! Can you believe it?"

"I was always meaning to speak to her," my mother said. "But I never had the time."

"Wait a minute!" I interrupted. "You mean the people who live directly across the street? They won the lottery?"

"That's right," my mother said. "Isn't it amazing? I've never known anyone who won the lottery before."

"You still don't," my father said. "You've never actually met them."

"I've waved," my mother corrected him, "as I was backing out of the driveway. That counts."

"Not for much," my father said.

"You mean," I continued in my astonishment, "the house across the street, the one with the FOR SALE sign?"

"That's the one," my mother said. "You can hard-ame them for wanting to move, now that they're and all."

Why should he turn out to be the one who gets rich?" my father lamented. "Of all the dumb luck! So close and yet so far!"

I couldn't stop asking the same question over and over. "Those people? That house? That driveway? The one you would come to next if you were driving down the street to our house in a car, or a school bus, or on a bicycle, or in A NEWSPAPER TRUCK?!!"

"What are you talking about?" my father said. "The house right over there. The one with the rusted tricycle in the bushes."

"Maybe I should bake them something," my mother said.

"I doubt they're hungry," my father responded. "Besides, they're leaving."

"Yeah," I said, "with my money."

"I'm sure everyone feels they should have won," comforted my mother.

I went to my room to complain to Orwell about being skunked again by fate. Obviously, the people across the street had wound up with a newspaper intended for me. Orwell must have put the winning numbers in my horoscope before he went in for his operation, not knowing that my father had just canceled our subscription.

Rats, rats, and double rats! What good was luck if it kept missing you all the time?

88

The meaning of money

Sitting in my room with Orwell, agitated about the loot landing at the wrong house, I eventually recalled the rabbit's recent dream suggestion to try to see things in a different light. And so, with reluctant effort, I forced a revised theory to percolate in my brain.

What if what was happening wasn't events going haywire? What if what was happening was happening according to plan? What if I was never supposed to get the money? What if Orwell never walked again?

Nature thrives on change. But is all change merely random? Just because something is unpredictable doesn't mean it's an accident. Just because we can't figure out a pattern doesn't mean it happened by chance.

Everything keeps changing all the time — dreams, weather, neighbors. And I had heard, possibly in church, that nothing changes everything like money does. I had even heard it said that sudden money can make you worse off than you were before you had it, but how this could be true, I couldn't see.

I thought about a conversation I'd had with my father, not so very long before, when together we'd dragged our after-Christmas trash bags to the curb.

"Look at that!" my father said.

"Look at what?" I replied.

"Look how many trash bags we've put out on the curb."

"There's a lot," I observed.

"Look up and down the street," he continued. "Did you happen to notice that we have more trash bags out here than anybody else in the neighborhood?"

I hadn't noticed, but it was true. We had a handsome little mountain of them.

"Do you know what this means?" my father asked, but I didn't, so he told me, as I knew he would. "It means that you and your sister got more things for Christmas than anyone else in the neighborhood, that's what it means."

"Oh," I said.

"It means," he concluded, "that you and your sister should be very grateful."

But to tell the truth, I wasn't. I was glad when I got the presents, of course. Who wouldn't be? But by the time my father and I'd tossed those trash bags on the curb, the happy holiday feeling the presents brought was long gone.

I'd much rather have Orwell hopping and healthy and hanging around than a whole roomful of store-bought presents. I looked at him. He nibbled politely on a carrot. Orwell was starting to get a real bedridden look. His hair was a mess. I rummaged around in a desk drawer and found an old doll hairbrush that I never use anymore, part of a set I'd gotten for Christmas when I was my sister's age.

I lifted Orwell out of the cage ever so carefully and set him in my lap.

I have no idea what happened to the doll, but I can still remember begging my mother to get it. All those times I was sure I had to have something, only to discover after I'd gotten it, I didn't really want it after all!

Over the years, I've accumulated so much stuff this way, stuff that now jams the drawers of my desk, clutters up my bookshelves, spills from the top of my closet, and lies forgotten in the shadows underneath my bed. Useless junk. Stupid toys. Disappointing gadgets that don't work. So many different kinds of things that someone made and someone sold and someone, namely me, just had to have.

You know what I think? I think that if something is for sale, then the person who is selling it has figured out that it isn't that important after all. So maybe I shouldn't buy it either.

The stuff that really matters is never for sale. It just shows up, sometimes in your front yard.

I brushed that sad sack of faint life lying so limply in my lap. Soon, his fur began to take on a sheen, becoming a rich and earthy brown, like the hair of bears lolling in the shade in summertime, or countless armored acorns scattered among autumn leaves. It was a bold brown, like the hard bark of winter trees defiant in the snow. A shimmering, glistening brown, like the tight, wet fur of water mammals working tirelessly on the riverbanks in the spring, nature's brown, a manly brown, a brown that quietly warns of hidden strength.

Where else had I seen this color, tousled and shining in the sun?

A movie with a message

Winter and the woodpile both were nearly gone. The snow that fell on Saturday melted into raindrops before it could reach the ground. I brought in the last of the hickory logs and laid them in the fireplace, where they complained hissing and sizzling to the kindling, but eventually took full responsibility for the flame.

My father had rented a video for the evening. My mother baked oatmeal-raisin cookies. My sister insisted on turning out all the lights, the better to imagine being at the movies. I flopped down on the floor on a pile of pillows I'd pilfered from the couch.

The movie was the story of a family that sets out on a journey to make a new life. Some of it was funny. Some of it was sad. Some of it I didn't understand. It made me think of Orwell and how he'd wandered far to make his home with me.

I must have been pretty tired, because when it was over, instead of jumping up like I always do and heading off to do something else, I stayed on the floor as the credits rolled.

I never usually look at movie credits because I never know who those people are. They might as well be lottery winners, as far as I'm concerned. But as the tiny white letters went whizzing by, one name among them caught my eye. "Orwell Lapin," it read. "Second unit assistant to the associate director."

Interestingly, *lapin* is French for rabbit. Even so, I would have dismissed this sighting as a coincidence, had it not been for the message that followed Mr. Lapin's name. Before disappearing into the top of my television screen, it said,

FEELING BETTER THANK YOU
THANK GRANNY TOO.

"What?" I said. "Did you see that?"

The sputter of the fireplace was the sole reply. The others had already left the room. I stopped the tape, rewound the credits, and played them back again. There was no Orwell Lapin to be found.

Had I imagined it?

Or had Orwell begun leaving me messages the way my mother used to do, back during all those years when I was little, at my old school, hiding notes in my books and my lunch box and pinned inside my coat?

Had there been other vanishing messages that I had missed? Messages like my mother's "You're a great kid — I love you" and "Here's a bunny hug — be good today" scrawled into the fog of a frosted windowpane early on a winter day or drawn in the dust beneath my feet?

I advised my brain to pay closer attention.

A purloined paper

The weekend passed with little else to remember it by. The church was dressed in purple to mark the countdown to Easter. My father and my mother worked on the house. In a brief, closely supervised experiment, my sister and I let her cat climb inside Orwell's cage.

Orwell didn't seem to mind.

On Monday, the people who lived across the street became the people who never were. A moving van, painted with the outline of an ancient sailing ship, backed into their lucky driveway with great lurching trucklike squeals, explosive hisses, and loud self-important clatters as I was heading off for school. It was gone with their stuff before I got back home.

The people across the street had high-tailed it out of there like people in a hurry. They left a birdbath, garden tools, and a perfectly good trampoline standing in their backyard. They left hoses attached to their faucets. They left trash cans on the curb.

The rusted tricycle that had lain undisturbed in their front bushes for the better part of a year continued its nesting for a few days more, until a real estate man in a dark blue suit wrestled it out one somber and drizzly morning and jammed it into the trunk of his car.

For several days I watched as newspapers piled up on the lawn. I don't take things that aren't mine. I never have and I never would. But even though I hadn't paid for these particular papers, I figured they almost belonged to me, and anyway, nobody else seemed to want them.

Crows rose with the sun the day I made a lightning dash across the street to my absent neighbors' house. The breaking dawn behind me reflected from the windows like nearly identical watercolors neatly arranged for sale, each made by painting magenta pink right on top of azure blue while the blue was very wet. Bathed in this heavenly light, I nervously knelt to scoop the papers into my arms.

They say someday you have to pay for all your sins. I say you start paying right away.

Two of the stolen newspapers were wet. I hoped it was from rain, but it could have been from passing dogs. In any case, the soggy pages shredded when I tried to turn them. Another paper, barely two days in the yard, had already become a habitat for spiders. I dropped it in a trash can the moment I got the news.

One paper remained. I flipped back to the comics page, spied the smile face on Scorpio's numbers and set to work deciphering. It soon declared

A FRIEND PAYS YOU AN IMPORTANT COMPLIMENT.

What friend? What sort of compliment? This didn't sound like Orwell. This was just an ordinary, luck-of-the-draw horoscope, and despite its goofy smile face, I had drawn a dud.

Oh, well. *C'est la vie!* I thought. That's life in the funny papers. I tossed the paper on the counter and prepared to feed my rabbit.

Whether Orwell's legs were improving, I couldn't tell, but his appetite certainly was. His demand for lettuce, celery, spinach, carrots, and radishes was beginning to be noticed.

"Shouldn't your rabbit be eating alfalfa pellets?" my mother asked, leading the family into the kitchen to forage for breakfast, just as I was attempting to leave.

"He doesn't like that stuff," I replied. "He likes fresh food."

"Fresh food is expensive," my mother pointed out.

"Many people consider rabbits to be fresh food," my father chimed in, picking up the newspaper I had provided.

"Ugh!" my sister said as she flopped into a chair. "Who would eat a rabbit?"

I withdrew from the discussion in order to deliver the goods.

I knew it was true that rabbits aren't well positioned in the food chain. Many creatures find them easy pickings. Clearly, when the world began, the luck of the draw hadn't gone their way. But surely there's a reason rabbits are the way they are. I mean, you have to believe in something, don't you? Even if it doesn't have a name.

A rabbit is an extraordinarily beautiful creature. Unlike a turtle or a spider or a moose, a rabbit is a delight to observe. A rabbit's fur, its ears, its nose, its tail — all are uniquely constructed and arranged. A rabbit's face is very pleasant. It makes you happy just to see it. A rabbit is soft and gentle and begs to be hugged. Just to touch one feels like love.

Maybe this is the reason a rabbit isn't very rugged, why it's "not put together especially well," as the new veterinarian had said. Maybe, to make a rabbit, God was willing to sacrifice durability for beauty.

In this respect, a rabbit has more in common with a painting or a poem or a symphony than with a rhinoceros or a horseshoe crab. To be sure, God made them all, but with the rabbit, he took his time.

It had to be: God sent Orwell to me.

In the sunlight streaming through the window by his cage, Orwell lifted his face from the vegetarian feast I'd prepared him, wiggled his nose appreciatively, and opened his mouth to release a tiny, rabbit-sized burp.

"You're welcome," I said.

A change in the weather

Back in the kitchen, the rest of my family was eating less nutritiously. Cereal. Juice. Lightly buttered toast. And for the grownups, coffee weakened with skim milk.

I sat across from my father, whose face was hidden by the paper I'd procured. He must have been reading the sports section, because the back of the sports section is where they put the weather, and it was the weather page that faced me as I poured Frosted Mini-Wheats into a bowl.

There is so much information on the weather page. There is a map with color-coded temperatures. A detailed forecast for the city, the area, the state, and the country for the day that lies ahead, plus a long-term guess for five. There are highs and lows for more than a hundred cities. Pictures, sort of like on a horoscope, showing the phases of the moon. Charts having to do with air quality, humidity, precipitation, river stages, lake levels, and what was going on outdoors a year ago today. There are even phone numbers to call to get more information!

Finally, there's a friendly little paragraph written by a weather forecaster about making the weather a part of your life — as if anyone could escape it! This time the paragraph was about lightning and how many times it kills people.

A university reported that three hundred unlucky people die every year from lightning strikes. The weather service said it's a hundred and six. The safety council said it's exactly one hundred. The national climate data center said it's only forty-one.

The weather forecaster said he didn't know which experts to believe, but even if the highest number were the one that's true, the odds of being killed by lightning were three million to one, better odds, he said, than your chance of winning the state lottery, where the odds on any given day are five million to one. Since I'd seen the lottery strike right across the street, is it any wonder that I'm a little jumpy during thunderstorms?

Then, as sudden as a bolt ka-blamming from the blue, brain lightning struck the breakfast table. I spied some words on the weather page that I'd failed to see before. Without warning or apology, I jerked the paper from my father's hand.

"Hey!" he said, spitting Grape Nuts on the table. "I was reading that!"

"Hold on a minute," I responded impatiently. "I'll give it back."

There it was, a single, tiny line of type, just above the giant ad for trucks and minivans, and just beneath the heading "Special Bulletin." Seven nearly microscopic words, like seven dwarfs, standing in a single line, saying

THE WAIT IS PART OF THE CURE.

There on the weather page I'd found a phrase in a familiar tone having nothing to do with the weather and everything to do with recuperating rabbits.

The paralyzed Orwell was on the move, jumping from the comics page and its superstitious horoscopes to the sports section's popular weather page.

On the move and moving up, on the rise in his personal career, Orwell was no longer to be found among fortunetellers. He had joined the ranks of the weather forecasters!

A twister of fate

Time leapt. February, the shortest month, like the shortest kid in class, was pushed aside by bully March.

Both Orwell and my days at school improved. In the mornings, I'd awake to find my rabbit occupying a different corner of the cage. He seemed proud of his achievement. At school, my teachers usually remembered me from the day before. I started sitting with the same two girls at lunch. They were kind of quiet, but because they were nice to me, I liked them.

Band, P.E., math, and English were a breeze. History had begun to interest me. Science class was cool. Soon we were to submit ideas for projects for the science fair. As for French, well, *mon chéri*, let me put it this way: Whatever grade I got wouldn't even count. The course for which I'd volunteered was just an entertainment.

The tousle-haired boy smiled when I passed him in the hall, but I couldn't tell if he was smiling like you would smile at a friend, or if he was smiling the way some people smile at people they feel sorry for.

But just as the fog was lifting on my junior high career, and barely two months after an extended Christmas holiday, they closed the whole school down for what they called Spring Break, even though winter was still hanging around.

Sometimes the world makes no sense. If you don't like something, it seems like you have to do it all the time. But when you start to like it, then you have to stop. Riding the bus home in the middle of the week, knowing that I wasn't going back to school for a while, I felt like I'd been fired.

Everything keeps changing all the time.

To help make ends meet, my mother took a job at the nearby junior college. To help pass the time while he waited for his luck to change, my father continued working on our house.

As Orwell's condition improved, his messages, published in the paper tossed across the street, became as prevalent as the weather. His pattern now included light observations:

WHAT YOU DO MATTERS LESS THAN WHY

mixed with warm requests:

ASK THE CAT TO COME BACK THURSDAY.

I was, of course, happy to accommodate him.

My sister and I were given household duties. Hers was laundry. Mine was cleaning up the rooms. I was issued an upright vacuum cleaner with a picture of a tornado stamped on its green plastic case.

In no time at all, I was cleaning up a storm. I've found that vacuuming goes much faster if you don't stop to move things out of the way. The only problem is the cord. Either it isn't long enough to reach where you want to go or it's too long and keeps getting wrapped around chairs and wastebaskets and lamps. But no job is hassle-free, so, like Lewis and Clark pushing relentlessly upstream on the great Missouri River, I persevered.

Not surprisingly, my room, which I'd saved for last, was the biggest mess of all. Books and papers and dirty clothes covered my unmade bed. Pieces of projects littered my desk and shelves. Pine shavings from Orwell's cage were scattered on the floor.

I plugged in, turned on, and went to work intent

on suctioning anything smaller than a dime. The carpet color began to return foot by hard-fought foot.

As I turned the L-shaped corner, the cord, stuck into the wall at the other end of the room, wrapped around the LEGO table that supported Orwell's cage. Not knowing this, and with the mission's end in sight, I gave it a firm tug to set it free, which is exactly what it did, taking the table, Orwell's cage, and the startled Orwell with it.

One thing always leads to another. Events always happen end to end. The cage landed on the floor, the door popped open and a rabbit-shaped bundle tumbled out onto the floor.

"OH, NO!" I shouted, "I'VE KILLED HIM AGAIN!"

But I had not.

All I had done with my carelessness that day was make a worse mess in my room and give my wounded rabbit the chance to step back into his cage, which, to my amazement, is exactly what he did.

Orwell didn't hop, as other, less-battered rabbits do. Instead, he raised himself up like an old man rising from a chair, keeping his knees bent, half-standing, half-squatting on his haunches, and in a single careful movement, he high-stepped over the hurdle beneath the open door into the familiar sanctum of his cage.

A miracle had taken place right before my eyes!

A surprise encounter

On the second day of Spring Break, the sun came out and so did Orwell.

While I practiced jump shots in the driveway with only occasional success, Orwell was rediscovering his feet. He stood in the front yard lifting his back legs one at a time in a slow unsteady march. On the mend, but not yet out of the woods, the little rabbit moved like he was wearing rented shoes several sizes too large.

A white sedan followed by a minivan pulled in across the street. The real estate man in the dark blue suit emerged from the car. Three people got out of the minivan, a slender, well-dressed woman, followed by a girl and a boy. The girl appeared to be my sister's age, perhaps a little younger. The boy I knew was my age, because it was the tousle-haired boy from school.

"Is that your rabbit?" he called to me.

"Sure is!" I called back. "His name is Orwell!"

"Funny," he laughed, carelessly combing his hair with his fingers. "Somehow I figured you for a monkey!"

As my brain scrambled to come up with a response, my basketball, a purple one from childhood days, spun from my hands and leapt into the street, where it raced down the hill in a sudden impulsive break for freedom.

I took off running to retrieve it. When I returned, out of breath, my heart in high gear, the tousle-haired boy and his companions were inside the empty house.

"Holy smokes, Orwell!" I said. "Do you suppose they're planning to buy that place?"

Orwell lifted his right foot and stared at it. Then he put it back down in the grass and lifted his left foot. He stared at it. He repeated this procedure several times. Finally, he put both feet down, raised his fragile body up into an elevated squat, and, in that comic high-step I'd witnessed once before, walked to where the grass, bleached and winter brown just days before, had started to return to green.

Orwell carefully nibbled off a slender shoot, swallowed it, then looked at me and nodded his head firmly before returning to his picnic.

"Wow!" I said. "*Quelle chance!*" What luck!

I stood and stared across the street, my eyes unblinking, mesmerized by the possibilities unleashed by this amazing coincidence. The tousle-haired boy, right across the street!

What a friend I had in Orwell!

Once again, my delinquent basketball slipped from my grasp. It bounced on the concrete driveway with a distinctive *tap-tap-tap-ta-tap!* and rolled harmlessly against the magic rabbit dining on the lawn.

Who gets the credit?

Who saved Orwell?

Was Orwell saved from permanent paralysis by the new veterinarian, with his experience and his skill in putting back together the pieces chance had torn asunder? Is he the one who deserves the credit? And if he does, shouldn't he share it with the person who invented the MRI?

My grandmother with her connections played no small part in fixing the rabbit's future. Orwell himself had noticed that.

I'm the one who found Orwell crumpled in the yard, the one who brought him in and fed him and kept him from the cold. I did my part to rescue the injured rabbit. I deserve recognition.

Others in my household have earned acknowledgment for helping, each in his or her own unique way. My father because he backed me up. My mother because she let him stay. My sister because she sneaked him carrots and twice helped me clean his cage.

Minor players helped Orwell by staying minor, thereby preventing worse effects: the Irish setter who captured Orwell but didn't eat him right away. The veterinarian who gave him shots and his first murky X-rays.

Obviously, nature played a major part in Orwell's fate. So did Orwell's luck, switching from bad to neutral to good, as it seemed to have done so far.

God made all the creatures, so, of course, he contributed, but even the smartest people in the world disagree over how deeply he gets involved.

Who saved Orwell? Who is responsible for *anything* that happens? People and events are all connected.

As Orwell, in a nutshell, once explained it all to me, "What you choose to do today matters."

A change of pace

Orwell's cage by the windows was now merely Orwell's bed. With its door remaining open, he was free to come and go as he pleased, using it only at night or when he felt like resting. Most often during the day, Orwell walked around the house with me, or went off on his own exploring, sometimes watching my father or my sister work, sometimes visiting the dog or cat.

Orwell's high-step way of walking really cracked me up. Have you ever rolled your jeans up as high as they would go and gone wading in a pond? You know how you lift your legs up very high before you set them down again, just a short step away? That's how Orwell walked from room to room, less like a rabbit than a living cartoon.

"Why does he do that?" my sister asked, emptying her laundry basket on the bed that I'd just made.

"Do what?" I said.

"Why does he walk like that? Why doesn't he hop like other rabbits?"

"I guess he can't," I answered. "Or maybe he's forgotten how. Anyway, what he's doing seems to work."

"I think it's weird," my sister said.

"'Weird' may be Orwell's middle name," I replied.

In an effort to hone my detective skills, I began keeping Orwell's written communications posted on my wall. Each day the list grew by seven words.

Orwell seemed very fond of words. In the afternoon, our chores completed and my father busy with his tools, my sister and I played Scrabble until my mother got home from work. Orwell never missed a game.

The curious rabbit would look at my letters, then stride over to see what my sister had drawn. He'd stand behind her in that peculiar, stoop-kneed way of his, scratching his chin, then he'd step back over to my side and wait until I played my hand.

Scrabble is a game that's played with seven letters at a time. The letters you can use depend on luck.

The words you choose to play rely on skill. Orwell's value to the game was mostly in the former. With him standing near, I drew lucky combinations every time: CAPSIZE. MAXIMAL. GIRAFFE.

"Your rabbit is cheating," my sister complained, when the score stood at 217 to 45.

"He can't help it," I explained. "It's in his nature. He likes to change the outcome."

"Well, tell him to go sit down," my sister said. "This isn't any fun for me." By way of illustration, she played the single letter O, creating the common two-point word ON. With Orwell's intervention, I promptly turned it into QUOTATION.

"That's it, I quit!" my sister said.

"Would you rather play cards?" I asked. "We could play seven-card rummy."

"No way," my sister said. "Not with that rabbit hanging around."

Orwell takes a powder

With occasional help from me, my mother, and my sister, and some emergency assistance from a plumber with a big white truck, my father had nearly finished the rooms that other workers had started on the back of our house so many months before.

I had finished my chores and was looking for Orwell. I wanted to discuss an idea for a science fair project that had come to me while gazing out our windows into the backyard, where at this moment the sun was shining brightly, robins were hopping in the grass, and pint-size black-and-white woodpeckers were walking up and down the trunks of trees.

Perhaps my rabbit would be interested in helping me demonstrate unique methods of animal locomotion.

I found my father standing on a ladder with a paint roller duct-taped to a broom handle, trying to reach the uppermost parts of a vaulted ceiling. To ventilate the fumes, he'd opened all the windows and the sliding double door that led to the deck.

"Have you seen Orwell?" I asked.

"He was just here," my father replied. "He's been watching me all morning. I figured he left to find you."

I checked with my sister. She hadn't seen him either. Nor was Orwell with the dog, whom I found on the floor in the family room sleeping, as usual. Orwell wasn't off conspiring with his new friend the cat, because the cat, like the dog, was taking an afternoon snooze, curled up in a shaft of sunlight in the dining room.

Worried now, I checked every room in the house, including closets and storage rooms. Orwell was nowhere to be found. It occurred to me that he must have gone outside.

I hurried back to the master bedroom to speak to

my father. He was teetering dangerously on the top of the ladder, leaning over backward with his roller apparatus, his face to the ceiling, his glasses covered with white spatters.

"When was the last time you saw Orwell?" I asked.

"Not sure," he grunted. A blob of paint, liberated from his roller by Earth's gravity, plopped onto my father's glasses like a gift from a low-flying goose.

"When was the last time you saw *anything*?" I wisecracked, dashing through the open door.

There were no rabbits on the deck, but I did find painted footprints leading out the door and down the steps. They were a funny kind of footprints, not like rabbits usually make. They were two-footed footprints, the kind a child might have made, if the child had walked through spattered paint and if its feet were like a rabbit's.

Any detective worth his salt would have known that they were Orwell's!

Orwell wasn't in the grass. He wasn't by the pond. He wasn't in or on the woodpile. He wasn't hiding in the bushes or behind the trees. He must have squeezed through the fence and gone into the park. But why? Why would Orwell run away, or walk away, as the case may be?

I opened the gate, ran down the steppingstones to the children's playground and on to the jogging trail, anxiously searching for my wayward rabbit.

Orwell was in no condition to be on his own. He couldn't run. He couldn't hop. He could only walk that crazy, high-stepping walk, which would hardly be enough to keep him out of danger.

If he was in the park, he wasn't where I could find him. I kept moving. Down the sidewalk, into other people's yards, down the street, my heart beating faster with each passing, bunnyless minute.

Where in the Sam Hill universe was Orwell?

Eventually, red-faced, frantic, and out of breath, I came to the boulevard where the traffic runs in a perpetual race to the expressway past the neon-lit windows of the Saturn-Mart, and there, out in the road beside the grassy median, I spied a flattened, furry lump.

My heart sank into my shoes. My mouth went completely dry.

Orwell?

I stood on the sidewalk and trembled, straining to see beyond the blurry stream of cars. It wasn't trash that someone had discarded from an open window. It wasn't a plastic bag the wind had carried from the Saturn-Mart. It wasn't carpeting, or a blown-out tire, or a single athletic shoe.

It was an animal, a small furry animal. And it was dead.

And it smelled bad. Really bad. Even worse than the exhaust fumes from the cars. As I stood there with my overloaded brain shooting sparks inside my skull, trying to make out the shape of the deceased, a whiff of it hit me full in the face.

I knew that stink. Everybody knows that stink.

Skunk!

The creature in the road, who was no more, was a skunk. Solemnly, I said a prayer for the poor, unlucky white-striped stiff. I said another one for Orwell. Wherever he had gone, thank God, it wasn't here.

An impossible case

The newspaper subscription, prepaid by the lottery winners who had lived across the street, ran out the very day that Orwell walked away.

Coincidence? Perhaps. In any event, its effect was that I had no contact with my rabbit. Not a sighting. Not a single word.

I was worried.

Worry had gotten into me like a fever. It sat in my stomach and it occupied my brain. It wouldn't go away no matter what I told myself, no matter how I tried to console myself by saying, "He's OK, he'll be back, he's just off exploring for a while."

Worry was waiting for me the moment I woke up. It followed me like a noise throughout the day, constant, grating, distracting.

At night, when my head sank into the puffy pillow that my grandmother had bought for me, I tried to make the worry go away by praying, but the persistent thought that somewhere out there my rabbit was walking upright to his doom, his knees bent, his body straight like a Cossack dancer, strolling blindly into death, denied me the comfort that prayer sometimes provides.

On the second night, there was a thunderstorm, a violent one, with lightning illuminating the sky. One especially impressive bolt shook the house when it crashed into a tree in the park. The winds blew hard. In the far distance, where sometimes I hear the sounds of trains, a tornado siren cried.

It was not the kind of night to be outside.

When Lewis and Clark pushed up the Missouri, across the Continental Divide and down the Columbia through the great forests of the Pacific Northwest, they endured every kind of weather I've ever seen. Surely a rabbit, born and raised outdoors, could make it through a night or two. Surely. That's what I told my brain to think about.

Where was Orwell? What was he doing? And how was I to go about finding him? Losing a wild rabbit is not like losing a dog or a cat. You can't post signs around the neighborhood or run an ad in the newspaper and expect to get results.

If ever a private detective were needed, I told myself, it was now.

I got out of bed and turned on the light. I sat down

at my desk with pen and paper and began to make a list.

EXPLANATIONS FOR ORWELL'S ABSENCE

1. Gone to seek his fortune.
2. Got lost while exploring.
3. Got bored and left.
4. Got mad and left.
5. Got feelings hurt and left.
6. Had to deliver a message.
7. Off on a secret mission.
8. Remembered something and went to get it.
9. Had to meet somebody. Be back later.
10. Playing a practical joke.

These were the most likely explanations that came to mind. Others, like "abducted by space aliens" or "kidnapped, held for ransom" I dismissed as being too far-fetched.

The problem with my list was that, because I had no clues, I couldn't with certainty eliminate any of it. The case of the disappearing rabbit was, as the French say, *impossible*. No real detective would take it.

I wondered, What if this had happened in a movie on TV? What would the movie detective do if he had no clues?

He'd question people, that's what he would do!

And the first person he would question would be me.

I sat at my desk in the middle of the night, an angry thunderstorm carrying on outside to beat the band, trombones and all, and began to question myself. "Try to think," I asked. "Did you notice anything unusual about the victim that day?"

"Everything about the victim was unusual," I replied. "From the moment he arrived in my yard."

"Very well, then. Let's try it a different way. Did anything happen that day that seemed strange?"

"Yes."

"What?"

"Everything."

"Try to be specific."

"All right. My father was painting upside down."

"Very good. Anything else?"

"My mother went to work and none of us knows what she does."

"Good. Good. Please continue."

"My sister and I have been turned into maids, school has been temporarily canceled because spring is just around the corner, and my rabbit walked out the back door, standing upright, with white paint on his feet. Is that strange enough, or shall I go on?"

Lightning flashed through the corner windows, illuminating Orwell's empty cage.

"Thank you very much," I told myself. "I will get back to you."

"But wait," I pleaded. "What about my rabbit? Can you find him for me?"

"I will do my best," I replied. "First, I must examine the clues."

"What clues?" I asked. "There aren't any clues."

"There are always clues," I insisted. "Everything that happens leaves clues. I just haven't found them yet." But I would, I vowed silently. I had to! I had come too far with Orwell to let him simply vanish from my life.

Perhaps if I gave my brain time to rest, I'd figure this one out. I switched off the light and climbed back into bed, remembering that somewhere I had heard it said, "Sufficient to the day is the worry thereof."

Spring moves in

Mourning doves scattered when I stepped into the front yard to inspect the starting of the day. Two fat squirrels clambered up to the roof. Robins, too busy to be disturbed, merely hopped aside as I walked by. In a raggedy circle surrounding the big tree, the first green evidence of daffodils peeked up from the earth like groundhogs checking out the sky. And coming down the street, big as a house and heading right where I was standing, was a moving truck.

I was getting new neighbors.

"A moving van just pulled up across the street," I told my family at the breakfast table. "I think I may know one of the kids."

"I should bake them something," my mother said.

"Good idea," my father agreed.

By the time I got back outside, the minivan had arrived and was parked at the curb. The moving truck was jackknifed across the driveway and out into the street, where it would have blocked a lane of traffic, had there been any. Double doors as big as the entrance to a garage were open in the back and on the sides. Two men were walking up and down ramps with big cardboard boxes that they stacked three high on the lawn. Even though the day had not yet warmed up and the men's work had just begun, they were sweating from the effort.

The front door to the house was open. From inside I heard a radio playing much too loudly and people laughing. I knocked politely on the door frame. *Tap-tap-tap-ta-tap!*

No reply.

With one foot, I stepped inside and leaned forward into the house, keeping the other foot outside on the porch, in order to make it clear to any observer that I wasn't barging in uninvited.

"HELLO?" I called. "Is anyone home?"

The only answer was the sound of the radio. The

laughter had stopped. I took a few steps into the house, stopping at the edge of the entry where the polished wood floor met the light green carpet of the living room.

"HELLO?" I called again, peering around the corner.

The radio continued its unwelcome noise. I took two more cautious steps in its direction.

"What are you, a burglar or something?" a voice behind me asked, startling me.

Embarrassed, I turned around to face the tousle-haired boy. He had his arms folded across his chest. He looked angry.

"Oh, hi!" I said. "I tried knocking."

"I could have you arrested, you know," he said.

"I'm sorry," I replied sheepishly. "I just wanted to welcome —"

"And you'd probably have to go to jail, maybe even do hard time. You know what hard time is?"

"No."

"It's where they put you to work until your sentence is up."

"Oh, look, I'm really sorry. I just came over to —"

"But I'm going to give you a break," he continued. "Instead of calling the cops and going through a trial and everything, I'm going to let you start serving your hard time right now. Do you know how to operate a vacuum cleaner?" His stern face broke into a big smile.

"Actually," I said, returning the smile with relief, "I've recently become something of an expert."

Shooting the breeze

When the people across the street won the lottery that was meant for me, I thought, *What rotten luck.* But now that they were gone and the tousle-haired boy had taken their place, and he'd begun shooting baskets with me in the driveway, I thought, *What great luck!*

The thing about luck is you have to stay tuned to see how it all works out.

I had even started to think that possibly there's no such thing as luck at all. If everything happens because of something else, if everything is connected end to end, then what looks like chance is really the result of countless individual decisions all taking place in a universe subject to the same natural laws.

The tousle-haired boy called it "destiny." He said things are meant to be. And the more we talked, the more I liked to hear what he had to say and the way his voice sounded when he said it.

I was in the driveway discussing Orwell's disappearance with my new neighbor, hopeful that two brains would have better luck at finding a rabbit than one.

"He's probably around here somewhere," he said, bouncing the basketball off the backboard into the net in a quick, clean one-two from the edge of the sidewalk. "Probably just doing what he has to do."

"What do you mean?" I asked.

"Well, look, it's nearly spring, and, according to what you've told me, he just suddenly got up and walked out the door. Except for him walking like he was wearing snowshoes, that sounds perfectly normal to me. For a rabbit, anyway."

"You think he had no choice?" I asked, puzzled.

"Try to think about it like a scientist instead of a pet owner and you'll understand. Rabbits can't help being rabbits, you know."

"I don't get it," I said.

"Where'd you say you kept his cage?" he inquired.

"In my room by the windows," I answered.

"So he was able to see outside, right?"

"That's why I put it there," I said. "I can see the whole backyard from my windows."

"And anything that might have hopped into it," he added, sinking another one with a near-silent swishing sound, signifying a perfect nothing-but-net shot.

"Oh," I said. "I think I'm beginning to understand."

"I'll bet there are lots of rabbits around here. It's a rabbity-looking kind of neighborhood, don't you think?" He smiled at me, then, with an effortless leap, arced the ball high into the air, where it looked like it was going to overshoot, but at the last moment it stopped, fell, spun around the rim and wobbled through the net.

"Well, I have seen other rabbits," I admitted.

"Didn't you tell me that cottontail rabbits only like to be with other rabbits when they're feeding or when —"

"Or when it's time to start a family!" I interrupted. "Of course!"

"Bingo!" he exclaimed, surprising me by missing his next shot by more than a foot. He nervously combed his hair with his fingers and grimaced. "Ooops!" he said. "Your turn."

A crash course in philosophy

Everything not only changes, I realized, everything *must* change. It's the Law of Commonplace Events. My plans for my personal career now included becoming a philosopher.

I chose this new path for several reasons. First, being a detective was getting me nowhere. Not only had I not figured out why Orwell came into my life, I had managed to lose the mysterious little rabbit in the process.

Second, I realized that I enjoyed thinking about things more than I enjoyed actually doing things. Some people might call this being lazy, but only because they can't tell how hard my brain is churning while the rest of me is sitting there looking comfortable.

Finally, recent developments in my life had put pressure on my philosophy to undergo some changes, too. This required additional thinking time, time that could most easily be freed up by abandoning my mediocre career in private investigations.

Non regret rien. I have no regrets, I told myself, demonstrating my revised way of looking at things. Such changes are not only *inevitable,* they are improvements. If we just paid closer attention to the details of our daily lives, nothing that happens to us would surprise us.

Take my father's accident, for example. In hindsight, it had to happen. How long did he think that he could stand on top of a ladder, ignoring the warnings clearly spelled out in orange and black letters on the top step just beneath his foot, and ignoring, too, the natural force of gravity?

"I find it interesting," I told him, practicing my philosophy as I sat beside him in the ambulance en route to the emergency room, "that only one letter separates 'paint' from 'pain.'"

"Please be quiet," my father said.

While my father's foot was being bolted back together, I checked out the hospital cafeteria. Surprisingly, I found it to be a cheerful place, brightly lit, not too crowded, with clean, plastic-topped tables and lots of good food. But, since I hadn't taken much money with me, I had to settle for a little box of Lucky Charms and a half-pint of milk.

I knew when I turned the box around to read the back, as I always do when eating cereal, that I had made the choice destiny had earmarked for me. Under the heading "Lucky You" was a drawing of a big-eyed comic leprechaun wearing a green top hat, shiny green jacket, green buckle shoes, and a huge, almost frightening smile. He was dancing and holding a pot of gold on which were written seven rabbitlike words:

HAVING A WONDERFUL TIME. BE BACK TOMORROW.

Unlike the silence surrounding his sudden departure, this time Orwell had thoughtfully sent me advance notice of his migrations.

My rabbit was coming home!

In books, stories have a beginning, a middle, and an end. In real life, they go on forever, because one thing always leads to another.

After proving that he could hobble around on crutches, my father was released from the hospital with a cast on his foot and a job offer in hand, having shared a room with a newspaper executive who was sympathetic to his injury and impressed with his credentials. My father had accepted his roommate's offer with the explanation that he couldn't start until he could walk, an outcome that could be some weeks away. The newspaper executive, whose nose was packed with cotton and covered with white tape, replied in a muffled voice that he understood completely and would be pleased to wait.

I am convinced that such a lucky turn of events is not a coincidence, if by coincidence you mean something that is unusual. Everything about our lives is based on such a coincidence. If what was going to happen were limited to what is probable, then not a single one of us ever would have been born. The odds are always against it. Evidently, unseen forces rule our lives.

One of those unseen forces tried to sneak back into the house.

As my father swung his damaged foot awkwardly beneath his crutches, struggling up the steps to our front door, a small, brown, upright rabbit-shaped creature wearily emerged from beneath the bushes beside the porch.

"Orwell!" I shouted. "Where have you been?"

Slowly and side by side, the two disabled mammals stepped into the house to join a family grateful to receive them both.

My father collapsed on the sofa and went to sleep, while Orwell, obviously worn out from his nights on the town, climbed slowly up the stairs and into his cage where he, too, curled up and summoned the train to slumberland.

"Mister," I whispered softly, lest I disturb the rabbit's

rest, "you've got some explaining to do."

Spilling the beans

To assist him in preparing for his new career, and to give him something to do while lying on his back on the couch with his foot propped up on pillows, my father instructed my mother to reinstate our newspaper subscription.

I resumed my ritual dash across the front yard each day to retrieve the paper, lingering in the increasingly bright mornings to read amid daffodils who waved their happy yellow heads at every passerby. But although I examined it closely every day, I found nothing in the paper that I could attribute to Orwell.

School also started up again and, with it, my interest in the science class I attended with the tousle-haired boy from across the street. It was strange how easily things worked out when it came time to choose partners for the science fair. I chose him and he chose me. Nobody laughed. Nobody teased. Nobody complained.

After school, we bounced around a basketball and a few ideas.

"Do you like rockets?" I asked.

"Not much," he said.

"Me neither," I said. "What about an experiment with seeds and plants?"

"Wouldn't that take a long time?" he asked.

"You're right. How about filtration? A filtration experiment wouldn't take very long," I suggested.

"Filtration? Of all the fascinating areas of science there are to choose from, you're interested in filtration?"

"What about weather? It's interesting."

"Too many variables," he responded.

"Maybe we should do something with food," I suggested.

"Now you're talking. Let's go check out your refrigerator."

"Really? You want to do a food experiment?" I asked, happy to have worked things out to his satisfaction.

"Of course not," he replied. "I'm hungry. Let's go eat while we figure out something that's never been done before. That's what I want to do. A scientific breakthrough! With nachos on the side!"

We passed my father sleeping on the couch. The newspaper was laid neatly across his chest. A headline caught my eye: GLOBAL SITUATION CHANGES AGAIN — FUTURE UNCERTAIN. *This,* I thought, *is what the newspaper business is all about.* Everything changes every day. The people who work at the newspaper simply write it down.

In the kitchen, we found Orwell leaning against the dishwasher eating lettuce. He looked up eagerly when we arrived.

"That's a cool rabbit," the tousle-haired boy said. "How did you teach him to stand up like that?"

"I don't teach Orwell. Orwell teaches me," I replied, popping some chips and cheese into the microwave oven.

"Huh?"

"Orwell is a very special rabbit," I said proudly.

"Sure," he said. "And your cat is a very special cat and your dog is a very special dog and these nachos, also very special, are soon to be history. Got anything to drink? Juice? Soda? Chocolate milk?"

I poured us each a big glass of orange juice, and with Orwell in the room listening without objection, told the tousle-haired boy everything I knew about the rabbit, his medical history, his language skills, his influence over games of chance. When I had finished, he pushed his empty plate aside and leaned across the table, his face just inches from mine, so close I could smell the lingering fragrance of the soap he'd used that morning.

"Now that's what I mean by scientific break-through," he whispered, beaming. Then, quickly standing up straight and combing his fingers through his hair, he added, "Assuming, of course, that what you say is true."

"Don't take *my* word for it," I said. "There are others around here who can convince you."

From over by the dishwasher came the sound of one paw clapping. *Tap-tap-tap-ta-tap!*

The riddle of the day

"When is a door not a door?"

"When it's ajar," I replied automatically. "That one's older than I am."

The tousle-haired boy and I were sitting on the curb, reading the comics in the early morning light as Orwell enjoyed breakfast on the lawn.

"It must be hard to come up with something new every day," he suggested.

"Well," I continued, "I never thought it was funny in the first place. Nobody I know ever says 'ajar.' Doors are either open or they're closed, you know? There's no middle ground."

"OK, let's try another one," he said. "When is a rabbit not a rabbit?"

"Let me see that!" I said reaching for his section of the paper. "That sounds like a message from Orwell! Or did you make it up?"

"I'm just trying to figure out what you've got here," he said, gesturing to the rabbit who was now walking upright, his head down, his arms behind him, inspecting the lawn like the old-time comic movie actor Groucho Marx. "Maybe he only looks like a rabbit."

"What do you mean?" I asked.

"I mean," he said, "that our bodies are not who

we are. We're stuck with them, of course, but inside, we're completely different. Don't you think so?"

"I never thought about it," I admitted.

"Take you, for example," he continued, "Just because you look like a monkey doesn't mean you are one." He looked up from the newspaper and smiled, his brown morning hair wilder than usual.

"'Thanks a lot,' said the kettle to the pot," I replied.

"Don't mention it," he said.

Neither of us spoke for a while. I traded him the sports section with its colorful weather page and prediction of another pre-spring snowfall for the two pages of comics he'd just finished.

"Maybe he's your guardian angel," he said.

"Orwell?" I asked.

"Sure," he said. "Everybody has one. Few people know what they look like, though."

"Do you have one?" I asked.

"Sure!" he said, as if I'd just asked him if he had a heart or a brain or feelings like other people.

"Do you know what your guardian angel looks like?"

"Not really," he said. "I used to think he might look like my father, but then I figured that would be too obvious. Angels are masters of disguise. He's probably found some other body to be in now. Maybe even yours."

"Oh," I said.

I put my hand on his shoulder and looked out at the streaks and cracks in the street that separated his house from mine. Except for the birds and squirrels and one distant dog walker at the far end of the street, we were the only creatures up and about.

Orwell arrived noiselessly and sat down between us as the sun rose in a magenta sky. After a long and reverent silence, the tousle-haired boy stood up, brushed off his jeans, and announced, "We better get ready for school."

Scientists at work

Constructing the experiment for the science fair presented the tousle-haired boy and me with a number of problems, the first of which was its classification. We had been given three categories to choose from: physical sciences, biological sciences, and Earth/space.

I thought our project should be listed as biological, since it featured a living rabbit, but the tousle-haired boy said he thought it should be physical, since the actual experiment we intended to conduct would be performed with inanimate Scrabble tiles.

Then I changed my mind and said maybe it ought to be Earth/space, since we were dealing with possibly unexplained phenomena, like UFOs, the ultimate Earth/space connection.

My partner said that was possibly so, but what we really had was a fourth category, a super category, one that governed all the other categories. He suggested that we solve this problem by checking all three boxes on the District Science Fair and Festival official entry form.

"A single classification is too limiting for something this big," he said.

The next problem we had to confront was the problem itself, that is, the statement of the problem, posed as a question, that would permit us to construct a scientific experiment that would yield a clear and persuasive answer.

I suggested, "Can a rabbit change your luck?"

The tousle-haired boy said that wasn't specific enough. He suggested, "Does the presence of a lucky rabbit change the outcome of a game of chance?"

"That's what I just said!" I responded.

"No," he explained, "what I said was more scientific than what you said."

"Do it your way," I grumbled. "It makes no difference to me."

We decided to skip over the recommended step of reviewing all the published scientific literature in the field, because, as my partner pointed out, "What literature? How many rabbits like this can there be?"

This saved us a lot of time.

The next step was to express a hypothesis. Since I'd been living with the experiment's one and only variable for some time, I came up with this one. It was, "It is hypothesized that when a lucky rabbit enters the room, the laws of probability go out the window."

"Very creative," my partner said to my great satisfaction, offering no changes or objections.

We decided to conduct the actual experiments over a number of days. We wanted to be sure that we didn't wear out Orwell with too much work at once, and we hoped to eliminate the possibility of the outcome being affected by a lucky day, which everybody has now and then.

Since smile faces on horoscopes never run more than four days in a row, I figured five days of experiments ought to be enough to eliminate the lucky day variable.

My partner said he thought it was possible to be lucky forever, but, even so, five days of doing the same experiment over and over seemed like plenty. He also mentioned that he'd like to fix himself a sandwich.

We abandoned planning for the day and prepared PB&J on wheat bread with potato chips and fat-free devil's food cookies. We washed it all down with tall glasses of cold milk.

"Next time," he suggested, wiping his lips with a paper towel, "we should fix the food before we start."

The amazing Orwell

That weekend, my mother finished painting the master suite, and with the help of my sister and myself and our three new neighbors from across the street, my mother and my temporarily hobbled father moved into their elegant new quarters.

Since I am the firstborn child, I was offered my parents' old bedroom first, but even though it was a bigger room and faced the front, I declined this once-in-a-lifetime opportunity.

I like my L-shaped room with its view of the entire backyard and the neighborhood park beyond. I like the way it divides itself with a perfect right angle into two distinctly different parts. I like the way my furniture and my possessions are arranged, offering, at a single glance, a history of my life and interests.

My room suits me just fine.

My sister was very pleased with my decision. Having unexpectedly been given title to a much bigger storehouse, she quickly made it her life's mission to fill it up.

That the master suite was finally finished after so

many trials was remarkable enough, but events, like the weather, keep changing in surprising ways.

When I asked my parents what their plan was for the room my sister had abandoned, they shared a sudden, conspiratorial look. My father, obviously unprepared, cleared his throat as if to speak, but it was my mother who hesitatingly spilled the beans.

"We're going to fix it up for the new baby," she said.

New baby? *Holy smokes!* I thought. What next?

This was a prolific time for Orwell, too. The tousle-haired boy and I had decided to perform six pairs of experiments on each day of the five-day series. Each experiment would include placing all the Scrabble tiles into an empty mayonnaise jar, shaking it thoroughly, then removing seven tiles from the top, one at a time, carefully recording each letter in a notebook.

First, we would perform it without Orwell. Then, we would invite the rabbit into the room and repeat the experiment just as before. We would do this six times a day, twice in the morning, twice after school, and twice before bedtime, until we had recorded the results of thirty identical paired experiments, a number sufficient, we believed, to persuade all skeptics.

As it turned out, it was also an opportunity for Orwell to advance his publishing career.

The first seven letters extracted from the mayonnaise jar were DYRAOGT.

"Well, that's useless," the tousle-haired boy said. "Now let's try it with the rabbit."

"Wait a minute," I said. "If you rearrange the letters you can make it say GOT YARD."

"And?" he asked impatiently.

"And that might be meaningful," I insisted.

"I don't think we should rearrange the letters," he said. "That would be interfering with the results."

"It could also be RYG TOAD," I said. "Or TYG ROAD or even ARTY GOD."

"We have a school bus to catch," my partner advised. "Get the rabbit."

I never had any doubt that Orwell would be able to demonstrate his unique abilities, but some people, and at least one rabbit, seem to do more with opportunity than others. Orwell is among those who are destined to exceed everyone's expectations.

The collection of wooden rectangles clattered cheerfully as I shook them up and down in the big glass jar. One by one, my partner removed seven letters from the top and laid them side by side until he had spelled out the word SIXTEEN.

"It's a number," I said excitedly.

"Interesting," the tousle-haired boy observed.

"Maybe he's going to give me another chance to win the lottery!" I cried.

"Let's continue with the experiment," my partner

advised.

I asked Orwell to step outside the room while we did another drawing *sans lapin,* without rabbit. This time the random results were EHAEEER.

"Nothing there," my partner said.

"There sure are a lot of *E*'s," I observed.

"That's to be expected," he replied. "It's the most common letter in the alphabet and the most common letter in Scrabble by far. There are twelve *E*'s in the game, three more than I and twice as many as *T, R,* or *N.* This is consistent with the laws of probability. Now bring the rabbit back in."

I found Orwell in the living room visiting the cat. "Can you come back in, Orwell?" I asked him politely. "We need your influence over the universe again."

In no time, Orwell's presence had produced the word MAGICAL.

"This is so cool," the tousle-haired boy announced.

That afternoon Orwell added two more words, RABBITS and WEARING.

The rabbitless control experiment turned up the blank tile plus IMOLSG on the first round and MIIPTIL on the second.

"Maybe we should have removed the blank tiles," I said.

"Well, it's too late for that now," my partner said. "Once it's started, we can't change the procedure."

After dinner, we conducted the third group of experiments. Orwell seemed to be enjoying himself, giving us SCARLET and FLOWERS.

Without him, we drew PIPERVL and IRNALLE.

"Aren't those the names of towns?" I asked.

"What?" he replied.

"Isn't there a place called Piperville? And Iranelle?" I asked.

"Give me a break," he said. "The rabbit is spelling out perfectly comprehensible seven-letter words. Look at this: SIXTEEN MAGICAL RABBITS WEARING SCAR-LET FLOWERS. Incredible! Meanwhile, the mayonnaise jar is coughing up gibberish. This is Nobel Prize–winning stuff. Don't mess it up."

"It was just an observation," I said, my feelings bruised.

"You know what your trouble is?" my partner said. "You think too much."

The amazing Orwell resumed his performance on Tuesday, the second day of experiments, by adding the words DANCING, QUIETLY, BENEATH, EMERALD, SHOWERS, and RAINBOW to the output the tousle-haired boy and I recorded in the notebook.

At the same time, his randomly produced competition came up with YFHSLI blank, ENOLAIW, OEATIID, ZUOROOC, ITUISOU, and YD blank OO blank W.

"This just gets better and better," my partner said, happily munching on a carrot stick he'd swiped from a bowl that I'd set out for our test subject.

On day three of the Orwell experiments, as the tousle-haired boy and I shared a stack of pancakes in the kitchen, I said, "I think Orwell is showing off. I think it's because of you and all the attention he's getting."

"Maybe he has an unrequited urge," he replied.

"Huh?" I said, accidentally putting my elbow into a blob of syrup, an oversight that later caused me to board the school bus with a napkin stuck to my denim jacket.

"You know, a need to write this stuff," he explained. "Driven by his inner voice."

"If you say so," I said.

Orwell's experiments that day produced RABBITS, TURNING, LIGHTLY, WISHING, SINGING, and TELLING.

The control experiment yielded O blank SVGSW, XEITDEN, RMFSIUO, DLEEFIW, ODFRKRC, and IA BLANK ERWN.

"That's the second time he's used the word 'rabbits,' " I said. "It must be important to him."

"Duhhh!" the tousle-haired boy mocked, gently scratching Orwell's head as the rabbit slept in my partner's lightly freckled arms.

Thursday's entry included HOPEFUL and STORIES and the number SIXTEEN again, followed by BASHFUL, BAFFLED, and RABBITS.

This was a sharp linguistic contrast to IRDYOH

blank, IUIHRDP, STNOEMR, DRNIEDS, RZASTGO, and RONLOIT.

"What if Orwell is controlling both sides of the experiment?" I wondered aloud. "You know, in order to make himself look better."

"So what?" my partner replied, ketchup dripping from the crisp, brown French fry he held between his thumb and his forefinger. "It just makes us look better, you know?"

It was a good thing that Friday was the last scheduled day of the science fair experiments. The pace of the testing and the excitement generated by the results had worn everybody out, humans and beasts alike. Orwell responded to our morning summons by dragging himself listlessly into the room.

"That bunny looks like he's had it," the tousle-haired boy observed.

"Maybe we pushed him too hard," I said, worried.

The results, however, suggested it was worth the effort. Whereas the unassisted, random drawing had created ANQNENR, NDDUDTE, IYYAAHD, HRESEOE, ORE-AOLI, and HDG blank OJN, Orwell's last words from the mayonnaise jar were SMILING, BRIEFLY, BETWEEN, SHADOWS, KNOWING, and NOTHING.

Outside, a thin sliver of a moon was visible through the kitchen window. A star, or perhaps it was a planet, glowed nearby like a child's night-light. The wind, quiet all day, had picked up until it was gusting intermittently, randomly rattling a loose window screen.

Seated at the kitchen counter leaning over the spiral notebook in which we had painstakingly recorded our week's work, my partner pushed his unruly brown hair from his forehead and smiled.

"Your rabbit has written a poem," he announced. "In thirty consecutive attempts, without missing a beat, this amazing creature has produced a beautiful poem consisting entirely of seven-letter words."

As he spoke, Orwell leaned against the wall, crossing both his arms and his feet in a pose of modest abandon.

"Listen," he said, reading to me in a most pleasant and soothing voice:

SIXTEEN MAGICAL RABBITS
WEARING SCARLET FLOWERS
DANCING QUIETLY
BENEATH EMERALD SHOWERS.
RAINBOW RABBITS TURNING LIGHTLY
WISHING
SINGING
TELLING HOPEFUL STORIES.
SIXTEEN BASHFUL, BAFFLED RABBITS
SMILING BRIEFLY BETWEEN SHADOWS
KNOWING NOTHING.

"Man!" I said.

"Usually," my tousle-haired partner responded. "But in this case, it's definitely rabbit."

An intriguing who-dunnit

St. Patrick's Day, the first day of spring, my sister's birthday, my parents' thirteenth wedding anniversary, the one hundred ninety-third anniversary of Lewis and Clark's departure from Fort Clatsop, marking the beginning of the intrepid explorers' long journey home — time tripped along on many milestones.

Intrigued by my rabbit's artistic achievement, I began to read poetry in my spare time, hoping to figure out what Orwell's feat was all about, if, indeed, the poem was his.

Had Orwell done this?

Choosing Scrabble letters from a jar, had Orwell constructed coherent verse from thirty words of equal length? As preposterous as this would seem to someone just arriving on the scene, I had no other explanation.

If the newspaper is to be believed, stranger things are happening every day. And if the many histories recorded in the Bible have it right, the extraordinary has been commonplace since time began. Clearly, there is a point at which the improbable becomes inevitable. But who is responsible for a poem?

Is some great creative life force the author, using a man or a woman, or possibly even some lesser creature, as its instrument? If so, is this true for every poem, or only for the good poems?

Is Orwell's poem a good poem, or is it only a good poem for a rabbit? Is Orwell inspired, or is he merely clever? As my afternoon dabbling in French had taught me so well, there is always more than one way of looking at things.

My personal career as a philosopher was off to a trying beginning.

Whatever else the poem may have been, it was also a turning point for Orwell's communications with me. As had happened before, his messages stopped. This time, however, proved to be more than an interruption. It seemed the little rabbit had shot his wad. Although we continued to understand one another's wishes and moods, that day Orwell's secret seven-letter messages ceased forever.

His life's work apparently complete, Orwell retired, becoming, by every appearance except his peculiar gait, an ordinary rabbit.

Hard to believe

"I can't believe it!" the tousle-haired boy said angrily, using a phrase that reminded me of my mother in earlier days. "This is so irritating!"

In his hand my partner held a four-page judging form from the District Science Fair and Festival. Out of a possible eighty-eight points, we had received a miserable fifty-six, a score equal to a letter grade of D.

All things considered, it was not a very good showing.

"They didn't believe us!" he wailed. "They said, listen to this, 'Rather than adhere to the scientific method of inquiry, your experiment seems to ridicule it.' What jerks! This makes me so mad!"

I looked at the score sheet. The only thing the judges really liked was the artistic presentation and workmanship of our exhibit.

I had drawn a picture of Orwell in his distinctive, upright pose, with a smile on his face and a twinkle in his eyes. Together, the tousle-haired boy and I had painstakingly colored it in with colored pencils. We had glued on actual Scrabble tiles so it looked like Orwell was standing on them. But we got clobbered on our hypothesis, our procedure, and our conclusion, and were served big fat goose eggs for our missing review of literature and our nonexistent bibliography.

"This is so typical!" my partner ranted on. "You make an authentic scientific breakthrough and nobody believes you! What's the use?"

"Well," I said, staring at the row of zeroes on the

last page. "Maybe if we'd read up on it first. *'Il faut étudier pour avoir de bonnes notes.'* It is necessary to study in order to have good grades."

"You're defending them?" he snapped.

"No," I said. "Just trying to see it another way."

Of course I was disappointed, but I could understand why people would be skeptical of a versifying, fortunetelling, moonwalking rabbit picking letters from a jar with his brain.

"I think people look for what's familiar," I suggested. "If it's different, they figure something's wrong with it."

"Maybe you're right," he said. "Maybe we're just ahead of our time."

"The first explorers," I added.

"With only a rabbit to guide us," he said, laughing.

Talent is recognized

During the week that led to Easter, red-and-yellow tulips bloomed in the backyard garden over the grave shared by the goldfish and the frogs. Tiny green leaves no bigger than a rabbit's nose twitched in the breeze that wafted through the branches of the hedgeapple tree.

At school, to our complete surprise, the tousle-haired boy and I were advised that we were to share first-place honors in the annual District Young

Writers' Competition. Orwell's poem had been entered on our behalf by a sympathetic science fair judge, who, unlike her colleagues, had found another way of looking at things.

So far, the pipeline that runs underneath the fields has not blown up, at least not in that spot, but an item in the newspaper that landed in my front yard reported that a pipeline *had* exploded hundreds of miles away, in a place where few people lived, shortly after suppertime. No one was hurt, but a seventy-year-old man who witnessed the accident was quoted as saying, "It was like the day of reckoning."

My father recovered fully from his accident. When he started his new job at the newspaper, my mother quit hers to prepare for the arrival of the new baby.

Since everything is connected end to end, the woman who was teaching me French quit to take the job my mother gave up. The last words she taught my class were, *"Tout est bien qui finit bien,"* which means, "All's well that ends well." This is a useless phrase, as far as I'm concerned, since nothing really ends, it just keeps on changing.